B49

KT-557-573

ROTHERHAM LIBRARY

KIVETON PARK

BRINSWORTH DINNINGTON

- - SEP 2011

2 9 OCT 2011

- 9 FEB 2012

- 5 MAR 2012

1 3 APR 2012

1 9 JUN 2012

- 6 AUG 2012

9/12

3 NOV 2012

8 - DEC 2012
1 4 JAN 2013

CENTRAL

3/13

10/13

2 8 OCT 2013

1 4 APR 2014

1 3 OCT 2014

MALTBY

10/14

2 3 NOV 2014

This book must be returned by the date specified at the time of issue as
the DATE DUE FOR RETURN.
The loan may be extended (personally, by post, telephone or online) for
a further period if the book is not required by another reader, by quoting
the above number / author / title.

Enquiries: 01709 336774

www.rotherham.gov.uk/libraries

THE FAR SIDE
OF PARADISE

ROTHERHAM LIBRARY &
INFORMATION SERVICES

B490966497

R00054679

THE FAR SIDE OF PARADISE

BY
ROBYN DONALD

All the characters in this book have no existence
outside the imagination of the author, and have
no relation whatsoever to anyone bearing the same
name or names. They are not even distantly inspired
by any individual known or unknown to the author,
and all the incidents are pure invention.

All Rights Reserved including the right of
reproduction in whole or in part in any form.
This edition is published by arrangement with
Harlequin Enterprises II BV/S.à.r.l. The text of this
publication or any part thereof may not be reproduced
or transmitted in any form or by any means, electronic
or mechanical, including photocopying, recording, storage
in an information retrieval system, or otherwise, without
the written permission of the publisher.

® and TM are trademarks owned and used by the
trademark owner and/or its licensee. Trademarks marked
with ® are registered with the United Kingdom Patent
Office and/or the Office for Harmonisation in the Internal
Market and in other countries.

First published in Great Britain 2011
by Mills & Boon, an imprint of Harlequin (UK) Limited,
Large Print edition 2011
Eton House, 18-24 Paradise Road,
Richmond, Surrey TW9 1SR

© Robyn Donald 2011

ISBN: 978 0 263 22211 1

Harlequin (UK) policy is to use papers that are natural,
renewable and recyclable products and made from
wood grown in sustainable forests. The logging and
manufacturing process conform to the legal environmental
regulations of the country of origin.

Printed and bound in Great Britain
by CPI Antony Rowe, Chippenham, Wiltshire

CHAPTER ONE

STONE-FACED, Cade Peredur listened again to the tape of his foster-brother's final call—a frantic, beseeching torrent of words recorded just before Peter Cooper killed himself.

'Cade, where are you? Where the *hell* are you—oh, with Lady Louisa, I suppose. Damn it, Cade, I need you more than any woman could—why aren't you home? *Why can't you be there for me?*'

A short pause, broken only by his breathing, jagged and irregular, and then, 'Cade, I've been such a fool—such an idiot.'

Not a muscle of Cade's face moved at the sound of choked weeping.

At last Peter said in a thick, despairing voice, 'Taryn was my last—my *only*—hope. It hurts—so bloody much, Cade, so much...' Another wrenching pause and then, in a voice Cade had never heard before, Peter said, 'There's nothing left for me now. She laughed when I asked... *laughed*...'

The silence stretched for so long that when he'd first heard it Cade had been sure the call was over.

But eventually his brother whispered, 'It's no good, Cade. I'm sorry, but it's no good any more. I can't—I just can't live with this. She's gone, and she's not coming back. Tell the parents I'm sorry to be such a useless son to them, but at least they'll still have you. You're the sort of man they wanted me to be, and God knows I tried, but I've always known I didn't have what it takes. Get married, Cade, and give them some grandchildren to adore. They'll need them now...'

He stopped abruptly. Then he said unevenly, 'Try not to despise me, Cade. I love you. Goodbye.'

Cade switched off the tape and walked across the luxurious room to look unseeingly across the London cityscape, fighting to control the rush of blind rage threatening to consume him. The call had come eight hours before he'd arrived home and by the time he'd got to Peter's apartment his brother was dead.

Peter had worshipped him, emulated and envied him, then finally grown away from him, but Cade had always been intensely protective of his younger brother.

Hands clenching, he turned and walked into his office, stopping at his desk. The photograph on it had been taken at his foster-parents' fortieth wedding anniversary a few months before Peter's death—Isabel and Harold Cooper all smiles for the camera, Peter's grin revealing a hint of feverish excitement.

As always, Cade was the odd one out—taller than the other two men, his features harsher and his expression unreadable.

His brother's suicide shattered that secure, tight family unit. A fortnight after the funeral, Harold Cooper had died from a heart attack, and while Isabel was still trying to come to terms with the wreckage of her life she'd stepped out into the path of a car. Onlookers said she'd moved as though in a daze.

She'd wanted to die too, but not before she'd

begged Cade to find out what had driven her son to suicide.

He'd held her hand while she'd whispered painfully, 'If…if I knew why…it wouldn't be so bad. I just want to *know*, Cade, before I die.'

'You're not going to die,' he said harshly. 'I'll find out what happened.'

Her lashes had fluttered up again, revealing a spark of animation in her gaze. 'Promise?'

To encourage that hope, that flicker of determination, he'd have promised anything. 'I will. But you have to keep going for me.'

She'd managed a pale smile. 'It's a deal.'

That had been the turning point; valiantly she'd gathered her reserves and struggled back to cope with everything life had thrown at her. It had taken months of rehabilitation, and she was now adjusting to living the rest of her life in a wheelchair.

The letter Peter had left for his parents lay in its envelope on Cade's desk. He flicked it open and read it again. Unlike the telephone call, it was free of overt grief. Peter had told his parents he loved them, that he was sorry to cause them pain, but his life was no longer worth living.

No mention of the woman who'd reduced him to this depth of despair. He'd never introduced her to his family, only spoken of her once or twice in a casual, throwaway fashion. The last time he'd gone home—to celebrate his first big commission as a sculptor, a work for a public park in a market town—he hadn't referred to her.

So why that anguished, cryptic mention in his final call?

Cade turned away, his hard, arrogantly contoured face set. What part had Taryn Angove played in Peter's death?

Had something she'd said, something she'd done, precipitated his final, fatal decision? It seemed possible, although she'd left for her home country of New Zealand eight hours before Peter's suicide.

Cade had always known that revenge was a fool's game; he'd seen the hunger for it eat into the intellect, destroy the soul.

Justice, however, was a different matter.

Progress had been infuriatingly slow. He knew

now her return to New Zealand had been organised well before Peter's death. He knew she and Peter had been good friends for almost two years, almost certainly lovers.

He knew Peter's bank account should have been flush with a large advance to buy materials for his commission. Indeed, the money had arrived—and immediately a substantial sum had been taken out and paid directly to Taryn Angove. But the rest of the money had been siphoned off in large weekly cash payments, so that when Peter had died there had only been a few hundred pounds left.

If—and it was only an *if*, Cade reminded himself—Taryn Angove had somehow got her hands on it all, that could be why Peter had killed himself. Unfortunately, so far there was nothing, apart from that initial payment, to connect her with its absence.

But now, thanks to dedicated work by his security people, he knew where she was in New Zealand.

Cade looked across at the suitcase he'd just finished packing. His arrangements were all made and his actions from now on would depend on the woman he was hunting.

All day it had been still, the horizon a hazy brushstroke where simmering sky met burnished sea, the forest-clad hills around the bay drowsing in the fierce glare of a sub-tropical sun. Cade narrowed his eyes against the intense light to watch seabirds made dumb by the heat fight silent battles over their catch.

Even the tiny waves on the shore were noiseless; all he could hear was the thrum of thousands of cicadas vibrating through the forest-covered hills behind the bay—the prevailing summer sound in this long northern peninsula of New Zealand.

The sibilant hum was penetrated by the imperative summons of his cell phone. Only his personal assistant had that number, so somewhere in his vast holdings something had gone wrong.

From halfway around the world his PA said, 'A few matters pertaining to this meeting in Fala'isi.'

'What about it?' Because of his business interests in the Pacific Basin, Cade had been asked to attend a gathering of high-powered Pacific dignitaries to discuss the future of the region.

Dealing with that took a few minutes. His voice a little tentative, Roger, his PA, said, 'Lady Louisa called.'

Arrogant black brows almost meeting across the blade of his nose, Cade said, 'And she wanted…?'

'Your address. She was not happy when I wouldn't give it to her. She said it was urgent and important.'

'Thanks.' Cade didn't discuss his private life easily, but he did say, 'We are no longer together.'

A pause, then, 'You might need to work on convincing her of that.'

His voice hard and cold, Cade said, 'Ignore her.'

'Very well.'

Cade's mouth curved in a sardonic smile. Louisa wouldn't follow him to New Zealand—it was completely out of her orbit. His *ex*-lover craved luxury and fashion and the heady stimulation of admiration. This remote paradise couldn't satisfy her need for the envy of others.

'Ah…not to put too fine a point on it, but she sounded stressed.' Roger paused. 'Actually, desperate.'

Her father had probably refused to pay a bill. Cade shrugged broad shoulders. 'Not your problem.' Or his. 'How is your daughter?'

His PA hesitated before saying in a completely different tone, 'We hear the results of the first lot of tests tomorrow.'

What the hell did you say to a man whose child could be suffering a terminal illness? 'If you need leave or any help at all, it's yours.'

'I know. Thanks—for everything.'

'No need for thanks—just let me know what I can do.'

'Thanks. I will. Keep in touch.'

Cade closed down the cell phone, his eyes flinty. Against the fact that a three-year-old could be dying, Louisa was a very minor consideration. A sensuous, satisfying lover until she'd decided Cade—influential, moving in the 'right' circles and exceedingly rich—would make the ideal first husband, she'd been careless enough to let him overhear as she discussed her plans on the telephone.

It had needed only a few questions in the right ears for Cade to discover she'd run through most of the fortune inherited from her grandfather. With no chance of support from a father whose income had been decimated by financial crisis, marriage was the obvious solution.

Like Louisa, Cade didn't believe in the sort of love poets wrote about. However, although experience had made him cynical, he intended to marry some day, and when he did it would be to a woman who'd value him for more than the size of his assets. He'd choose carefully, and it would last.

Cade's expression hardened. If Louisa was desperate enough to follow him, he'd make sure she understood that he was not and never would be a suitable husband—first, last or intermediate—for her.

After eyeing the hammock in the dark shade of one of the huge trees bordering the beach, he succumbed to an unusual restlessness that drove him down onto the hot amber sand. He stared out to sea for a long moment before turning. Only then did a drift of movement in the cloudless sky catch his attention.

Frowning, he stared at it. At first nothing more substantial than a subtle darkening of the blue, the haze swiftly thickened into a veil, an ominous stain across the sky.

In the grip of its severest drought in living memory, the province of Northland was under a total fire ban. The manager of the farm he'd rented the holiday house from had impressed on him that any smoke anywhere had to mean danger.

Muttering a word he wouldn't have said in polite company, Cade headed towards the house, long legs covering the ground at speed. He grabbed his car keys and cell phone, punching in a number as he headed towards the bedroom.

'I can see smoke in the sky,' he said curtly when the farm manager answered. 'South, and close— in the next bay, I'd say, and building fast.'

The farm manager swore vigorously, then said, 'Bloody free campers probably, careless with a campfire. OK, I'll ring the brigade and round up a posse from here. With any luck, we'll be able to put it out before it takes hold.'

Cade eyed the growing smoke cloud. 'I'll go over and see what I can do.'

'Man, be careful. There's a tap in the bay, but the creek's probably dry. If you've got a bucket there, grab it.' Possibly recalling that the man renting the farm's beach house was an influential tycoon, he added, 'And don't try to be a hero.'

Cade's swift grin vanished as he closed the cell phone. The smoke suddenly billowed, forming a cloud. Until then there had been no movement in the air, but of course the instant some idiot lit a fire the wind picked up.

The faster he got there, the better. He hauled on a long-sleeved shirt and trousers with swift, economical movements, then wasted precious moments looking for a non-existent bucket before giving up.

Not, he thought grimly as he got into the car, that a bucket would be much help, but it would have given him an illusory feeling of control.

He drove too fast along the track to the boundary

gate; unlocking it wasted a few more valuable seconds so he left it open to give the manager and his men easy access. Lean hands tense on the wheel, he swung the four-wheel drive onto a narrow public road that led to the next bay.

It took too long to manoeuvre his vehicle around the tight corners through thick coastal scrub that would go up like a torch the moment a spark got into it. When the car emerged into searing sunlight a glance revealed no tents on the grassy foreshore or beneath the huge trees—nothing, in fact, but an elderly car parked in the deep shade cast by one of those trees.

And a woman in a skimpy bikini far too close to an area of blazing grass.

What the hell did she think she was doing?

Putting his foot down, Cade got there as fast as he could. He turned the vehicle, ready for a quick getaway, and was out of the car and running towards the woman before he realised she was directing a hose at the flames.

Tall and long-legged and young, she had a body guaranteed to set a man's hormones buzzing in anticipation. Smoke-smeared and glistening with sweat, she exuded unselfconscious sensuality.

At that moment she turned, pushing back a mane of copper-coloured hair that had been fanned across her face by the hot wind from the flames.

A flame flared up only a few inches from her feet and she jumped back, water from the hose splashing gleaming legs that went on forever.

The woman was crazy! Couldn't she see she wasn't achieving anything except putting herself in danger?

Cade covered the ground between them in a few seconds, watching the woman's expression turn to undisguised relief.

She thrust the hose into his hands and commanded brusquely, 'Keep directing it anywhere the flames try to get away. If they make it to those bullrushes the whole place will go up. I'll wet my towel and have a go at it from the other side.'

'Get dressed first,' he suggested, turning the pathetic dribble of water onto the flames.

She gave him a startled look, then nodded briskly. 'Good thinking.'

Taken aback and amused by her air of command, Cade watched her race across to her car to haul on a pair of inadequate shorts and a T-shirt and jam her feet into elderly sandshoes. Only then did she sprint down to the waves to wet her towel.

A sudden flare almost at his feet switched Cade's attention, but as he sprayed water onto it he wondered why on earth he was bothering. It was a losing battle; a wet towel would be as useless as the meagre trickle from the hose. Yet clearly the woman had no intention of giving up and doing the sensible thing—getting out of there before the fire made retreat impossible.

Cade admired courage in anyone, even reckless, blind courage. She might have lit the fire, but she was determined to put it out.

When she came running up from the shoreline she thrust the heavy, sodden towel into his hands. 'I'll take the hose—you're stronger than me so you'll be more efficient with this. Just be careful.'

The next few minutes were frantic. And hopeless. Working together, they fought grimly to hold back the flames but, inch by menacing inch, the bright line crept closer to the stand of bull-rushes, pushing first one way and then, when frustrated, finding another path through the long, dry grass.

'Get back,' Cade shouted when flames suddenly flared perilously close to those lithe bare legs. Two long strides got him close enough to put all his power into beating it out.

'Thanks.' Her voice sounded hoarse, but she didn't move, directing that inadequate spurt of water with a stubborn determination that impressed him all over again.

She looked down at the towel, which was beginning to scorch. 'Go down and wet the towel again.'

'You go.' Cade thrust the towel into her hands and grabbed the hose from her.

Sensibly, she didn't waste time in protest, turning immediately to run across the sand.

His foster-mother's influence was embedded so deeply he couldn't evade it, Cade thought wryly, stamping out a tuft of grass that was still smouldering. Women were to be protected—even when they made it obvious they didn't want it.

He glanced up the hill. No sign of the fire brigade yet. If they didn't appear damned soon he'd grab the woman and, if he had to, drag her away. It would be too late once the bullrushes caught; they'd be in deadly danger of dying from smoke inhalation even if they took refuge in the sea.

Panting, she ran up from the beach and almost flung the dripping towel at him. Her face was drawn and smoke had stained the creamy skin, but she looked utterly determined. Clearly, giving up was not an option.

Cade said abruptly, 'The brigade should be here soon,' and hoped he was right.

His arms rose and fell in a regular rhythm but, even as he beat out sparks along the edge of the fire, he accepted their efforts were making very little headway. No way could they stop the relentless line of fire racing through the grass towards a stand of rushes so dry their tall heads made perfect fuel.

If they caught, he and the woman would have

to run, but not to the cars. The beach would be their only refuge.

Once the fire got into the coastal scrub it would take an aerial bombardment or heavy rain to put it out. The cloudless sky mocked the idea of rain, and a helicopter with a monsoon bucket would take time to organise.

And if the wind kept building, the blaze would threaten not only the beach house he'd rented, but the houses and barns around the homestead further up the coast. Cade hoped the farm manager had warned everybody there to be on the alert.

A muted roar lifted his head. Relief surged through him as the posse from the station came down the hill on one of the farm trucks, almost immediately followed by two fire engines and a trail of other vehicles.

'Oh, thank God,' his companion croaked, a statement he silently echoed.

Taryn had never been so pleased to see anyone in her life. Smoothly, efficiently the firemen raced from their vehicles, the chief shouting, 'Get out of the way—down onto the beach, both of you.'

She grabbed a bottle of water from her car and

headed across the sand. Without taking off her shoes, she waded out until the water came up to her knees, and only then began to drink, letting the water trickle down a painfully dry throat.

Heat beat against her, so fierce she pulled off her T-shirt, dropped it into the sea and used it to wipe herself down. The temporary coolness was blissful. She sighed, then gulped a little more water.

The stranger who'd helped her strode out to where she stood. 'Are you all right?' he demanded.

He was so tall she had to lift her face to meet his eyes. Swallowing, she said hoarsely, 'Yes. Thank you very much for your help.'

'Go easy on that water. If you drink it too fast it could make you sick.'

Taryn knew the accent. English, clipped and authoritative, delivered in a deep, cool voice with more than a hint of censure, it reminded her so much of Peter she had to blink back tears.

Not that Peter had ever used that tone with her.

The stranger was watching her as though

expecting her to faint, or do something equally stupid. Narrowed against the glare of the sun on the sea, his disconcerting eyes were a cold steel-blue and, although Taryn knew she'd never seen him before, he looked disturbingly familiar.

An actor, perhaps?

She lowered the bottle. 'I'm taking it slowly.' Stifling a cough, she kept her eyes fixed on the helmeted men as they efficiently set about containing the flames. 'Talk about arriving in the nick of time!'

'I wouldn't have thought the village was big enough to warrant a fire station.'

A note in his voice lifted tiny invisible hairs on the back of her neck. He was very good-looking, all angles and strong bones and lean distinction. Not exactly handsome; that was too neutral a description for a man whose arrogantly chiselled features were stamped with formidable self-assurance. His aura of cool containment was based on something much more intimidating than good bones. An odd sensation warmed the pit of Taryn's stomach when she met his gaze.

Unnerved by that flinty survey, she looked

away, taunted by a wisp of memory that faded even as she tried to grasp it.

'They're a volunteer group.' She took refuge in the mundane and held out her bottle of water. 'Would you like some?' Adding with a wry smile, 'I've wiped the top and as far as I know I have no diseases you need worry about.'

'I'm sure you haven't,' he drawled, not taking the bottle. 'Thanks, but I've already had a drink—I brought my own.'

Stick to social pleasantries, she told herself, rattled by a note in his voice that came very close to mockery. 'Thank you so much for helping—I didn't have a hope of stopping it on my own.'

'Didn't it occur to you that lighting a fire in the middle of a drought could be dangerous?'

No, not mockery—condemnation.

Controlling an intemperate urge to defend herself, Taryn responded evenly, 'I didn't light it. I came down for a swim but before I got that far I noticed someone had had a fire on the beach above high tide mark to cook *tuatua*—shellfish. They didn't bother to put it out properly with sea water so I hosed it down, but a spark must have lodged somewhere up in the grass.'

'I see.'

Nothing could be gained from his tone or his expression. Stiffening, she said coldly, 'As soon as I saw smoke I rang the emergency number.'

'Ah, so that's why they arrived so quickly.'

Screwing up her eyes in an effort to pierce the pall of smoke, she said, 'It looks as though they're winning, thank heavens.'

Heat curled in the pit of her stomach when her gaze met his, aloof and speculative. Something in his expression reminded her she'd been clad only in her bikini when he'd arrived. And that the shorts he'd ordered her to get into revealed altogether too much of her legs.

Shocked by the odd, primitive little shiver that tightened her skin and set her nerves humming, she looked away.

He asked, 'Are you a local?'

'Not really.' She'd lived in the small village a mile away during her adolescence.

'So you're on holiday?'

Casual talk between two strangers abruptly hurled together…

Taking too deep a breath of the smoky air, she coughed again. 'No.'

'What do you do?' He spoke idly, still watching the activity on the grass behind the beach.

'I'm a librarian,' she responded, her tone even.

The brows that lifted in faint surprise were as black as his strictly controlled hair. In an abrupt change of subject, he said, 'Should you be swimming on your own?'

Taryn parried that steel-blue survey. 'This is a very safe bay. I don't take stupid risks.'

How did this man—this *judgmental* man, Taryn decided—manage to look sceptical without moving a muscle?

In a bland voice, he said, 'Fighting the fire looked risky enough to me. All it needed was a slight change of wind and you'd have had to run like hell to get to the beach safely. And you probably wouldn't have saved your car.'

That possibility had occurred to Taryn, but she'd

been more afraid the fire would set the coastline alight. 'I can run,' she said coolly.

His gaze drifted down the length of her legs. 'Yes, I imagine you can. But how fast?'

His tone invested the words with a subliminal implication that summoned a swift, embarrassing heat to her skin.

That nagging sense of familiarity tugged at her again. *Who was he?*

Well, there was one way to find out. Without allowing herself second thoughts, she said coolly, 'When it's necessary, quite fast,' and held out her hand. 'It's time I introduced myself—I'm Taryn Angove.'

CHAPTER TWO

CADE's heart pounded a sudden tattoo, every nerve in his body springing into instant taut alertness. This young Amazon was *Taryn Angove*?

OK, so courage didn't necessarily go with attributes like compassion and empathy, but she was nothing like the women Peter usually fell for. They'd all been startlingly similar—slight and chic, with an intimate knowledge of fashion magazines and the latest gossip, they'd pouted deliciously and parroted the latest catchphrases.

Cade couldn't imagine any of them trying to put out a fire, or throwing commands at him.

Mind racing, he took in the implications.

Did she know who he was?

If she did, she'd suspect that although this meeting was a coincidence, his presence in New Zealand wasn't. So she'd be wary...

Chances were, though, that Peter wouldn't have

spoken of him. An unpleasant situation some years before, when Peter's then lover had made a determined play for Cade, meant that Peter rarely introduced his girlfriends to his family. He'd once admitted that although he referred to Cade occasionally, it was only ever as his brother.

Cade knew the value of hunches; he'd learned which ones to follow and which to ignore. One was warning him right now to keep quiet about the connection.

'Cade Peredur,' he said smoothly, and shook Taryn Angove's outstretched hand. 'How do you do?'

He could see why Peter had fallen for her. In spite of the smoke stains, she was very attractive—beautiful, in fact, with fine features and creamy skin set off by coppery hair.

Not to mention a lush, sinfully kissable mouth…

Ruthlessly, Cade disciplined an unexpected kick of lust. Nowhere near as easily affected as his brother had been by a lovely face and lissom body, it exasperated him that Taryn Angove had a definite and very primal impact on him.

Which he had to suppress.

His investigation team hadn't been able to turn up a single person who wasn't shocked and astonished by his brother's death. The police had been unable to add anything beyond the fact that there had definitely been no foul play.

Peter had taken Taryn Angove to the theatre the previous night. She'd stayed with him that night and then he'd delivered her to Heathrow for the flight home. He'd cancelled an appointment with friends the following evening, but he'd spoken by telephone to them and he'd seemed perfectly normal.

Yet only a few hours later he'd killed himself.

From New Zealand, Taryn been asked to do a video interview with the police, but it revealed nothing; she hadn't mentioned anything that might have upset him, so they didn't consider her a person of interest. Although sympathetic, for them there was no doubt that Peter had committed suicide, and so there was nothing to investigate.

So she was the only person who might be able to help Cade find out why Peter had done it.

And there was the question of what had happened to the money…

Looking down into the wide green-gold eyes lifted to his, noting their subtle darkening and the faint flush visible even under a patina of smoke, Cade decided a change of tactics could be in order.

He'd come here determined to use whatever weapons might be necessary to find out what she knew. He'd try appealing to her better instincts—if she had any—and, if that failed, then intimidation might work. Or paying her off.

Now he'd met her, he wondered whether such weapons would be necessary. Taryn seemed nothing like he had expected. In order to choose the best method of persuading her to talk, he'd have to find out what made Taryn Angove tick.

Which meant he needed to get to know her.

Ignoring the electricity his touch zapped across her nerve-ends, Taryn concentrated on his grip—firm but not aggressive and completely confident.

Just her luck to be sweaty and smoky, with stringy hair clinging to her probably scarlet face. How did he manage to look so…so much in control?

Not that it mattered. Too late, she remembered who he was—periodically, she'd seen photographs of him in the press and appreciated his sexy, angular impact. He was a big player in financial circles and appeared occasionally in the gossip magazines a flatmate in London used to devour.

In them, he was usually squiring a beautiful titled woman with very expensive taste in clothes.

When he released her hand she said calmly, 'Thanks so much for coming to help when you saw the smoke.'

Broad shoulders lifted again dismissively. 'It was a matter of self-interest.' At her enquiring look he enlarged, 'I'm holidaying in the next bay.'

Had he bought Hukere Station? She dismissed the idea immediately. High-flyers like Cade Peredur didn't invest in remote agricultural areas in New Zealand's subtropical north; they went to the South Island's glorious mountains. Anyway, he didn't look the sort to want a cattle station; from what she remembered, his interests lay in the cutthroat arena of finance and world-shaking deals. And sophisticated English aristocrats.

In that cool, slightly indifferent tone he told her, 'I saw smoke in the air so I came to see what I could do.'

Taryn looked past him and said with a shiver, 'I'm so glad you did. I wish the idiots who lit that fire could see what their carelessness has led to. The thought of all these pohutukawa trees going up in flames is horrifying. Some of them are over five hundred years old. In fact, Maori legend says that the big one along at the end of the beach was used to tie up the first canoe that ever landed here.'

His gaze followed her pointing finger. 'It looks old enough, certainly.'

Taryn shrugged mentally at his lack of enthusiasm. He was English, and on holiday— why should he share her love for the ancient trees? It was enough that he'd come to help.

'It will take a lot of time before this place gets back to its previous loveliness,' she said. 'It's such a shame. It's the only good swimming beach close to Aramuhu township, but no one will want to come here until the grass grows again.' Her nose wrinkled. 'It looks horrible and it smells beastly, and everything—and everyone—would get covered in soot.'

Cade accepted the opportunity she'd offered—whether deliberately or not, he couldn't tell. 'If you'd like to swim, why don't you try the beach I'm staying at?' He nodded towards the headland that separated the two bays.

Startled and a little wary, she looked up. Caught in an ironic blue-grey focus, she felt her pulse rate surge and automatically ignored it. 'That's very kind of you,' she said without committing herself.

'It seems only fair.'

For the first time he smiled, sending languorous heat curling through Taryn. 'Fair?' she asked, only just stopping herself from stuttering.

'You might well have saved the beach house from going up in flames—and me with it,' he replied, noting that the farm manager was on his way towards them with the fire chief.

Noted too, with something close to irritation, the swift appreciative glances both men gave Taryn Angove.

Not that he could blame them. Those shorts showed off her glorious legs, and her bikini top accentuated her more obvious assets; only a dead man would ignore them.

The thought no sooner formed in his mind than he realised how bleakly appropriate it was. A man as dead as Peter…

'Hi, Jeff.' The smile Taryn gave the farm manager was friendly and open, but the one she bestowed on the grey-haired fire chief sparkled with mischief. 'Mr Sanderson.'

The fire chief gave a brief grin. 'Why am I not surprised to find you trying to put out a fire with nothing more than a garden hose?' he asked in a not quite fatherly tone before turning to Cade.

The farm manager introduced them and, as they shook hands, Cade said, 'It didn't take you long to get things under control.'

Hugh Sanderson nodded. 'Easy enough when you've got the men and the equipment. However, I'll leave a gang here to keep an eye on it. Just as well you both kept at it—probably saved a lot of destruction. Do you know how it started?'

'Ms Angove's theory seems logical,' Cade told him. 'All I saw was smoke in the sky.'

She flashed a green-gold, glinting glance at him as she explained what she thought had happened.

'Yeah, that would be it.' The fire chief indicated the sign that announced a total fire ban. 'Some idiots think a fire on the beach doesn't count. Thanks for keeping it away from the bullrushes— although I damn near had a heart attack when I saw you two trying to put it out.' He transferred his gaze to Taryn. 'No more heroine stuff on my patch, all right? If that fire had got into the rushes you'd have been in serious trouble, both of you. You OK?'

'Fine, thanks.' Her radiant smile made light of smoke stains and sweat.

The older man grinned. 'You never were one for keeping out of mischief. Patsy was just saying the other day she hadn't seen you for a while. Come and have a cup of tea with us when you're in town next.'

Cade waited until they'd gone before asking thoughtfully, 'What sort of mischief did you indulge in?'

She flushed a little, but laughed before explaining, 'When we first came to Aramuhu I was twelve, and I'd spent the previous eleven years living with my parents on a yacht in the Pacific. Fruit grows wild in the islands and I was used to just picking something off the nearest tree whenever I was hungry. At Aramuhu we lived for a few months next door to Mr and Mrs Sanderson and one day I took a cherimoya from his orchard.'

'Cherimoya?'

'It's bigger than an apple, sort of heart-shaped with bumpy green skin. Cousin to a custard apple.' Her voice sank into a sensual purr. 'They have the most delicious taste in the world. My mother marched me over to apologise and offer to work to pay for it. Mr Sanderson decided I could weed the garden for an hour, but once I'd done that he gave me a bag of them to take home. Even when we moved to a new house he made sure we were supplied with ripe ones in season and he still likes to tease me about it.'

Cade wondered if that husky tone was reserved for fruit, or if she murmured like that when she made love. His body tightened—and then tightened again for an entirely different reason at another thought.

No doubt Peter had also found that sleepy, sexy note both erotic and beguiling…

In an ironic tone that banished the reminiscent softness from her expression he said, 'Ah, small town life.'

'Where everyone knows your business,' she agreed with a swift, challenging smile. She focused her gaze behind him and he looked over one shoulder to see a racy red car hurtling boisterously down the road.

When he turned back she was frowning, a frown that disappeared when she asked, 'Did you grow up in a big city, Mr Peredur?'

'I was born in one, yes.' When taken away from his mother, he'd been living in the stinking backstreet of a slum. 'I'm going back to the beach house now. The invitation to swim is still open.'

And waited, concealing his keen interest in her answer.

She hesitated, then said lightly, 'I'm sticky and hot and I'd love a swim, thank you. I'll follow you in my car.'

'Right.'

Taryn watched him stride towards his Range Rover, long legs carrying him across the sandy ground in lithe, easy paces.

In a word—*dominant*. He compelled interest and attention by sheer force of character.

The swift fizz of sensation in the pit of her stomach startled her, but what made her increase speed towards her own car was the arrival of the one driven by a journalist for the local newspaper, an old schoolfellow who'd made it more than obvious that he was angling for a relationship.

Although she'd tried as tactfully as she could to show him she wasn't interested, Jason didn't seem to understand.

She fought back an odd clutch of apprehension beneath her ribs when she saw the possessive gleam of his smile as he swung out of the car, camera at the ready.

'Hi, Taryn—stay like that and I'll put you on the front page.'

'I've done nothing—showcase the men who put out the fire,' she returned. From the corner of her eye she noticed that Cade Peredur had opened the door of his vehicle, but not got in; he was watching them across its roof.

'Babe, they don't look anywhere near as good as you do.' Jason gave a sly grin and lifted the camera.

'No.' She spoke more sharply than she intended.

He looked wounded. 'Oh, come on, Taryn, don't be coy—we'd sell a hell of a lot more issues with you in those shorts on the front page instead of old Sanderson in his helmet. How about coming out with me tonight? I've been invited to a soirée at the Hanovers' place and they won't mind if I bring along a gorgeous girl.'

'No, thank you,' she said, keeping her voice even and light.

'Going to wash your hair, are you? Look,' he said, his voice hardening, 'what is it with you? Think you're too good to go out with an old mate now, do you? I'm not trying to get into your pants, I—'

He stopped abruptly as a deep voice cut in. 'All right, Taryn?'

'Fine, thank you,' she said quickly, adding rather foolishly, 'Jason and I went to school together.'

'Hey,' Jason exclaimed, ever the opportunist, 'you're Cade Peredur, aren't you? Mr Peredur, I'm Jason Beckett from the *Mid-North Press*. Can I ask you a few questions about the fire?'

'The person to tell you about it is the fire chief,' Cade said evenly. He looked down at Taryn. 'You go ahead—I'll follow.'

'OK,' she said, fighting a violent mixture of emotions.

Cade watched her walk across to her car and get in, then looked down at the reporter. Yet another man smitten by Taryn Angove's beauty; he should feel a certain amount of sympathy for the good-looking kid even if he was unpleasantly brash.

Instead, he wanted to tell him to keep his grubby hands and even grubbier statements to himself, and stay away from her if he valued his hide.

Shrugging, Beckett said, 'Well, that's women for you, I guess.' He produced an ingratiating smile. 'Are you planning to buy Hukere Station,

Mr Peredur? I've heard rumours of development, a farm park...'

'I'm on holiday, nothing more,' Cade said evenly, nodded, and strode back to his vehicle.

In her car, Taryn took a deep breath and switched on the engine. The hot air inside the vehicle brought a moment of giddiness, but at least it wasn't too smoky. Grimacing, she looked down at her legs, stained and sticky with a vile mixture of sea water, perspiration and smoke. The swim she'd been promising herself all week had never seemed so desirable, but she should have said, *No thanks, Mr Peredur*, and headed back to the small studio unit that was her temporary home.

So why hadn't she? She turned the key and waited patiently for the engine to fire.

Partly because she'd wanted to get away from Jason. But more because she was curious—and that forbidden tug of response excited her as much as it alarmed her.

Her mouth curled into a wry smile as she eased the car up the hill. It would take a woman made of iron to look at Cade Peredur and not feel *something.* As well as innate strength and authority, he possessed a brain that had taken him to his present position. Add more than a dash of ruthlessness to that potent mix, and the fact that he looked really, really good...

Yes, definitely a top-of-the-list male.

But not a man any sensible woman would fall in love with.

Not that *that* was going to happen.

Bitter experience had taught her that although she could feel attraction, when it came to following through on it she was a total failure.

In a word, she was frigid.

Without volition, her thoughts touched on Peter, the jumble of shock and sorrow and bewilderment assailing her as it always did when she recalled his proposal—so unexpected, so shatteringly followed by his death. Guilt lay permanently in wait, making her wonder yet again whether her response had driven him to take that final, lethal step.

If only she'd been a little less incredulous—if she hadn't laughed—would he have made a different decision?

If she'd stayed in England as he'd wanted her to, instead of coming home, would she have been able to help him get over her refusal?

All those *if*s, and no answers…

The car skidded slightly. Feeling sick, she dragged her mind back to driving. Although the station road was well maintained, it still required concentration.

At Anchor Bay she pulled up and switched off the engine. Cade Peredur's big Range Rover stopped beside hers and he got out, appraising eyes coolly intent as he surveyed her.

Tall as she was, a little more height would be a distinct asset when it came to dealing with this man. Taryn tried to dissipate another tingle of sensation by collecting her bag. As she walked towards Cade she felt embarrassingly self-conscious. She glanced away, gaze skimming a huge flame tree to one side of the bay, and caught sight of the house.

It was a relief to be able to say something impersonal. 'Oh, the bach is still here,' she exclaimed. She'd half-expected some opulent seaside mansion, suitable for very rich holidaymakers, against the bush-covered slope that backed the lawn.

'Bach?'

'The local term for a small, basic cottage, usually by a beach or a lake.'

Cade said, 'Obviously you know the place.'

'When I was at school, the previous owners allowed the school to hold its camps here—it's a very safe beach. The bach was just a ruin then. Possums used to nest in the ceiling, and I've no doubt there were rats under the floor.' She looked around reminiscently. 'Over there, under that pohutukawa, when I was thirteen I was offered a cigarette by a boy I was madly trying to impress.'

'And did you accept it?'

She gave him a mock-scandalised glance. 'Are you kidding? My parents are doctors! I stopped trying to impress him right then.'

He smiled. 'Good for you. Would you like to see what's been done to the house?'

It was difficult to match the abandoned shell she recalled to the house now. It had been almost completely reconstructed, its stone outer walls repaired and the timber ceilings stripped and oiled so that they gleamed.

'It looks great,' Taryn said, gazing around the long living room.

Although it must have cost a mint to renovate, it didn't look glossy or smartly out of place. Comfortable and beachy and cool, it had shelves containing a large collection of books and some seriously good pictures hung on the walls. Somehow it suited Cade Peredur.

He said, 'There's a changing room and a shower in the cabana over by the flame tree. You can leave your bag and your clothes there—I'll join you in a few minutes and bring you down a towel.'

She summoned a bright smile. 'Thank you. And then I can prove to you how competent I am in the water.'

Cade's answering smile didn't soften his face. In fact, Taryn thought as she walked across the coarse warm grass to the beach hut, the curve of his firmly chiselled mouth had made his striking, hard-edged face seem both cynical and forbidding.

Safely in the small building, she wondered if

anything ever did soften those arrogant features. When he kissed…?

She tried to imagine being kissed by Cade Peredur. Heat sizzled through her at the thought, but she couldn't see his face softening into a look of…well, *love* was out of the question, but what about lust?

The word *soften* just didn't fit the man. In his world it took an intimidating blend of brains, courage and formidable will to reach the top of the tree. When he kissed a woman it would be as a conqueror…

Hastily, she stripped off her clothes, pulling a face as she discarded them. They smelt disgusting—a mixture of smoke and sweat. They looked horrible too, both shorts and T-shirt smeared with ashy smudges and black marks. Even her bikini stank of the fire.

So, probably, did her hair and her skin.

Blissfully, she washed it all off in the sea's warm caress. A few minutes after she waded into the water, she caught movement on the beach from the corner of her eye and inched her head around so she could watch Cade Peredur stride across the sand.

Her heart jumped, startling her. Formidably and blatantly male, he seemed like some potent, elemental figure from the dawn of time—sunlit bronze skin and a perfect male body showing off sleek muscles that proclaimed strength and energy.

Some of which she could do with right now. Deep in the pit of her stomach, that hidden part of her contracted and sent another hot wave of sensation through her.

Lust, she thought, trying to douse it with a prosaic and practical attitude.

Although she'd never experienced anything so powerful before, this keen urgency that alerted every cell, tightening her skin and making her heart race, was merely run-of-the-mill physical attraction.

And if she tried to act on it, she knew exactly and in humiliating detail what would happen next; it would vanish, leaving her cold and shaking with that familiar fear. But even those mortifying memories couldn't banish the shimmers of sensation that pulsed through her, stimulating and undisciplined.

She turned away when Cade dropped his towel and made a fluid racing dive off the rocks at the side of the bay. An unexpected wave caught her—unexpected because she was too busy drooling over the man, she thought furiously as she inhaled water. Spluttering, she spat out a mouthful of salt water and coughed a couple of times to clear her lungs, opening her eyes to see her host heading towards her, strong arms cutting through the waves.

Oh, how…how inane! She'd probably just convinced him she wasn't safe in a shower, let alone the sea.

Sure enough, he trod water when he reached her and demanded, 'Are you all right?'

The sun-dazzled sparkles of water clogging her lashes surrounded him with an aura, a dynamic charge of power that paradoxically made her feel both weak and energised at the same time.

'Fine,' she returned, only a little hoarse from the dousing. Her heart was thudding as though she'd swum several kilometres through raging surf.

Get a grip, she commanded.

The last time she'd felt anything remotely like this she'd been nineteen and amazingly naive. She'd decided it had to be love, and became engaged on the strength of it. What a disaster that had turned out to be!

But there was nothing girlishly callow about her response to this man. Her body throbbed with a dark, potent sexuality unlike anything she'd ever experienced before.

She'd deal with that later. Right now, she had to get herself back onto an even keel.

Somehow she managed to produce a smile and said the first thing that popped into her head. 'Race you to shore.'

Cade's brows shot up as though she'd surprised him, but he recovered instantly. 'You get a handicap.'

'OK,' she agreed.

However, even with the handicap, he beat her comfortably. At least swimming as fast and as hard as she'd ever done worked off some of that wildfire energy.

When she stood up he said, 'You're good.'

'I was brought up almost in the water,' she said, breathing fast. He too, she noted with satisfaction, was breathing more heavily than normal. She added, 'My parents love the sea so much they called me after it.'

'Taryn?'

'No, Taryn is apparently derived from an Irish word meaning *rocky hill*. I had an Irish grandmother. But my second name is Marisa, which is from a Latin word meaning *the sea*.'

He observed dryly, 'It's a very pretty name, but I don't think it would help if you got cramps and there was no one around to help.'

'I've never had even the slightest twinge of cramp,' she said defensively, extremely aware of the way water gleamed along the muscular breadth of his shoulders, highlighting the effortless power beneath the skin. 'Anyway, I know how to deal with it.'

'Those medical parents?'

'And a Pacific upbringing,' she said shortly. 'Want to know how it's done?'

He laughed. 'Like you, I've never had cramp, but just in case—yes, demonstrate.'

When he laughed he was really something, she thought confusedly. Trying to speak prosaically, she said, 'First you change your kick. That often works. If it doesn't, take a deep breath and float face down, then pull your leg up, grab your foot and yank it upwards.'

She demonstrated, glad to be able to hide her face in the water for a few seconds. When she'd finished, she stood up and said, 'That almost always does the trick, I'm told.'

But he wasn't going to let her off so easily. Bumblebees zoomed through her bloodstream when he scanned her face with hooded blue-grey eyes. 'And if it doesn't?'

'Assume the same position and massage the offending muscle,' she told him succinctly, taking a surreptitious step back before her brain scrambled completely, overcome by all that bronzed skin, sleeked by water and backed by muscles and hard male authority.

He laughed again, teeth very white in his tanned face. 'Fine, I'll accept that you can deal with cramp. Are you on shift work to be able to take the day off?'

The abrupt change of subject startled her. 'I'm not working right now.'

His brows met over the distinguished blade of his nose. 'Really?'

Was there a hint of disparagement in his tone? Taryn bristled. Parrying a keen, questioning look, she said with cool reserve, 'I've been overseas, and when I came back I took a job selling souvenirs to tourists. It's getting close to the end of summer and tourists are slackening off, so I'm no longer needed.'

'Is there plenty of work around here?' His voice was casual. 'The village looked to be pretty small.'

Aramuhu was small, and there were very few jobs. But her future was none of his business. 'I'm sure I'll find something,' she said dismissively.

He smiled. 'I'm sure you will.'

Something in his tone caught her attention. Their gazes met, clashed, and the glint of awareness in his eyes summoned an intense, elemental response from her.

Taryn forced herself to ignore the shiver scudding down her spine, the tingle of anticipation.

Her breath stopped in her throat and she had to fight an odd belief that those few seconds of silent combat were altering the very fabric of her life, fundamentally changing her so that she'd never be the same again.

This unexpected attraction *was* mutual. Cade felt it too and, if she were willing, he'd probably enjoy a light-hearted, temporary affair.

Taryn didn't do casual affairs—didn't do *any* sort of affair. She'd had more than enough of the stark embarrassment when men realised that, although she could shiver with desire, when it came to actually making love she froze.

Her impetuous youthful engagement had caused such fierce disillusionment she'd been left emotionally bruised, so wary she'd never allowed herself to feel anything more than friendship for the men she'd met. Over the years she'd developed effective methods of brushing off unwanted approaches, yet this time temptation whispered seductively through her.

She'd stay well away from him—not give herself any chance of weakening. Turning away, she dived back into the welcoming water.

CHAPTER THREE

CADE didn't follow her. Taryn told herself she should be pleased. She'd be prepared to bet her next year's income—always providing she had one, she thought uneasily—that on his home turf he'd be hip-deep in swooning women. He had to be in his early thirties and he wasn't married. Most men with his financial and personal assets would enjoy playing the field.

As she hauled herself up onto the rocks she decided acidly that when he did make up his mind to marry he'd probably choose a glamorous model or actress. After five years or so he'd divorce her and marry a nice girl from his own strata of society—whatever that was—who'd give him the required couple of children. And in his fifties he'd divorce the second wife and marry a trophy one thirty years younger.

And she wouldn't want to be any of those wives.

That thought made her grin ironically before she slid back into the water.

Half an hour later she'd showered and reluctantly got back into her smelly shirt and shorts, emerging from the luxurious cabana to meet Cade, his muscled elegance defined by clothes that made her feel like a ragamuffin.

Only for an instant. The appreciative gaze that skimmed her bare legs did considerable damage to her composure. How on earth could he convey leashed interest with one swift glance—a glance that set her treacherous blood fizzing?

Possibly she'd misread his attitude, because his voice was coolly impersonal when he asked, 'Would you like a drink?'

'No, thank you,' she said at once, squelching a pang of regret. 'I smell of smoke and I really want to get out of these clothes.'

And could have bitten her tongue out. Would he think she'd made an unsubtle proposition? If he said something about a Freudian slip she'd have to bite back an indignant reply in case he guessed what she'd been thinking.

But he was too sophisticated to take her up on her clumsy choice of words. Not a muscle in his face moved when he said, 'Then some other time, perhaps.'

'That would be nice.' Taryn thought in self-derision that platitudes were so useful for filling in awkward moments.

Then Cade's smile hit her like a blow to her solar plexus. It turned her thoughts into chaotic, disconnected responses—all of which indicated, *He is utterly gorgeous...*

And he knew the effect that smile had on the opposite sex too.

Calmly, he said, 'If you want to swim, come and do it here. Nobody is going to want to swim in the next bay for a while.'

'I... That's very kind of you,' she said automatically. Yet another platitude.

Of course she wouldn't accept. Yet some traitorous part of her couldn't help wondering if this surprising invitation was the first step in—what?

Nothing, she thought sturdily, but heat scorched

her cheeks and she hastily bent to pick up the bag containing her togs.

'So that's agreed,' he said calmly.

Taryn had never met another man with his uncompromising aura of authority and controlled, potent sensuality. She preferred her male companions to be interesting and unthreatening.

Like Peter.

That memory drove the colour from her skin. She produced a meaningless smile and said, 'Actually, it isn't, but it's very kind of you to offer, and I'll probably take you up on it.'

She got into the car, frowned as the engine took a sluggish couple of moments to power, waved with one hand and drove off.

Cade watched the elderly vehicle, its persistent rattle deepening his frown. It certainly didn't look as though she had all Peter's money; if she did, she'd have been able to buy a brand-new car. The amount he knew for certain she'd received wasn't enough for that.

Perhaps she was canny enough to save it.

Unfortunately, he didn't know enough about her to make any reasonable judgement.

But that, he decided, could be dealt with. If she needed a job, he could provide her with one for long enough to find out whether she was a money-grubbing opportunist...

Taryn stopped at the top of the hill to look down into the next desolate bay. One fire engine remained there and a couple of the firemen were checking the perimeters of the burn but, although wisps of smoke still drifted up, the fire had clearly been controlled.

No little red car, either, she noted. Her frown deepened. Jason was becoming rather too pressing, a nuisance.

But not dangerous.

Unlike the man she'd just left.

Dangerous? She gave a snort and muttered, 'He's a *businessman*, for heaven's sake.'

Tycoons Taryn had seen on television or in the news were sleek, well dressed and well manicured. The thought of them being dangerous anywhere but in the boardroom was laughable.

So what made her foolish mind fix on that word to describe Cade Peredur?

Instinct, she guessed,

And Cade had certainly *looked* dangerous when he was scotching those greedy tongues of flame. He'd used her wet towel like a weapon, flailing it with an economy of movement that showed great strength as well as determination.

Also, there had been something in his manner when he approached Jason that had indicated a formidable male threat—one Jason had recognised.

OK, Cade was dangerous, as any strong man could be. But he was in complete control of all that strength. And none of it was directed at her.

So she didn't have to worry or feel intimidated.

Images of his powerful body filled her mind. Water-slicked and gleaming, every long muscle lovingly delineated, he'd stolen her breath away.

Yes, her decision to see no more of him had been the right one. She glanced down, frowning at the sight of the tight fist pressed against her heart, and let her hand drop, spreading out the fingers before shaking them so they relaxed.

Plenty of women must have felt the same surging

chemistry when they set eyes on Cade Peredur. Some of them would have ended up in his bed.

'Lots, probably,' she said aloud to a fantail flirting its tail from a nearby bush as it kept its beady black eyes fixed on her.

Smiling, she confided, 'Men like Cade Peredur—men who positively *seethe* with masculine confidence—always know they've got what it takes to make a woman happy in bed.'

Unless she was inherently cold...

But not one of his lovers had managed to make their liaison permanent.

And when—*if*—she ever fell in love properly, with a man who'd understand her fear of sex and help her overcome it—she wanted permanence, a lifelong alliance like that between her parents. She wanted trust and equality and a family, laughter and commitment and security...

None of which immediately brought Cade to mind.

'So forget about this love business,' she told the fantail. 'Because I don't think the sort of man I want exists in this world.'

And she'd keep away from any more chance

meetings with Cade Peredur. Next time she was struck by the urge to go to the beach she'd slake it with a shower. She wouldn't have to keep it up for long; he had to have things to do and places to go—empires to run, worlds to conquer, women to overwhelm—so he'd soon leave New Zealand.

And, once he was gone, her life would return to normal. No chills, no cheap thrills when those hard blue eyes met hers, no shivering awareness of his sheer physical impact...

For several moments more she stood looking down at the blackened landscape, frowning at the ugly stain across the grass and the rank smell of incinerated vegetation.

Then she stiffened her spine and got into the car and drove back to the sleepout she rented in an orchard a few kilometres from the village. Basic but comfortable, it boasted a miniature kitchen and a slightly larger bathroom, and the wide terrace outside made up for the lack of space within.

Clean once more, and in fresh clothes, she picked up an apple from the bowl on the bench and dropped into the lounger to demolish the fruit, carefully not thinking of Cade Peredur.

She needed to find work. She'd quite enjoyed selling souvenirs to tourists, but the summer wave of visitors through the village had receded, leaving her behind.

Jobless and drifting…

Ever since Peter had killed himself, an aching emptiness made her question the value of her existence.

'Time to stop it,' she said out loud, and made a sudden resolution.

Drifting was for slackers, for losers.

It was more than time to find some direction to her life. Before she'd gone to the United Kingdom, she'd enjoyed her work in one of Auckland's largest libraries. In London she'd worked in a coffee shop run by a New Zealand friend until she met Peter. They'd clicked straight away and he'd introduced her to his friends—a very earnest, intense artistic circle who'd treated her as a kind of mascot.

Peter had even found her a new job; she'd been in her element cataloguing the immense library collected over fifty years by the deceased uncle of one of his acquaintances.

Although she and Peter had become close, there had been no sexual spark between them, so his proposal had come as a shock. She'd thought he was joking and burst out laughing.

Only he hadn't been. And then she'd had to refuse him as gently as she could.

His death had horrified her. She should, she thought wearily, have realised it wasn't artistic temperament that caused his bouts of depression, always followed by tearing high spirits. She had wondered if something was wrong, but it had never occurred to her that *she* might be the cause.

Assailed by questions for which she'd never know the answers, and bitter remorse at not handling the situation better, she'd come back to Aramuhu, the only place she'd ever really called home.

But there was nothing here for her, no answers. So now what? The future stretched before her, featureless and uninviting.

'I need to make a plan,' she said aloud, resisting an impulse to give up. Unlike her parents, she was not a born rover. Yes, she wanted some purpose in her life, and she'd like to settle somewhere like Aramuhu, with a steady job in a nice library.

Unfortunately, the village was too small to be able to afford a salaried librarian. Like the fire brigade, the busy little library was run by volunteers.

OK, so if she were Cade Peredur, how would she go about making a worthwhile life?

A list of all the things she had to offer would be a good start. 'So what's stopping you from doing that?' she asked the empty room, and got out of the chair.

The following morning she surveyed the list with a frown. It looked reasonably impressive—she hoped.

Much more impressive than the bank statement she'd just opened. It told her she had enough money to last for two weeks. Something perilously close to panic pooled icily beneath her ribs.

Ignoring it, she sat down and wrote at the bottom of her list: *Stay here?*

That had to be her first decision. Living was cheap in Aramuhu—but the sleepout was used for kiwi fruit pickers in season, so it was temporary.

She could stay there for another couple of months, perhaps.

She could go to her parents in Vanuatu, but she had no medical skills, and they didn't need a librarian or even a secretary. Besides, it would only ever be a stopgap.

Frowning, she added a final few words: *If so, disengage from Jason.* Not that he seriously worried her, but she was beginning to feel uneasy at his refusal to take no for an answer.

An abrupt summons from the telephone startled her.

Not Jason, please.

'Yes?' she said cautiously.

And recognised the voice instantly when he said, 'Cade Peredur here.'

How did he know her number? Her stomach tightened when he went on without pausing, 'Do you have decent computer skills?'

Startled, she glanced at her ancient laptop. 'They're not bad.'

'I've just been called to a business meeting at very short notice, and I need someone to assemble and collate information for me from the

Internet and possibly transcribe notes. Would you be interested?'

That crisp, deep voice showed no indication of any interest in her but the purely businesslike. 'Well, yes,' she said cautiously.

'You are still looking for work?'

'Yes, but…' Taryn gathered her scattering wits and took a deep breath as that forbidden word *dangerous* appeared in red letters across her brain. Common sense demanded she say no, and mean it.

'What's the problem?' he enquired.

Pushed, she responded tersely, 'None, I suppose, if I discount the fact that we met for the first time yesterday, and I don't know very much about you at all.'

There was silence, as though she'd accused him of some deviant behaviour, before he said, 'I can probably come up with a reference. Who would you like to give it?'

Flippantly, she returned, 'How about the Prime Minister?'

'United Kingdom or New Zealand?'

Funny man.

Or seriously influential. 'Oh, don't bother,' she retorted. 'Where is this business meeting?'

'Fala'isi.'

An island basking in the tropical sun… Firmly, she pushed back memories of halcyon days. 'I didn't realise it involved travel.'

'Have you a current passport?'

'Yes, but—'

'It's only a short flight from Auckland.'

Fala'isi was a small island nation known for its good governance, safety and lack of corruption. However, she said, 'There are good temping agencies in Auckland—'

'It's a long weekend,' he said evenly. 'I've tried, and everyone's away on holiday.'

Of course, it was Anniversary weekend. Torn, Taryn wavered.

Into the silence, Cade said with cool, crisp detachment, 'I can assure you I have no designs, wicked or otherwise, on you, your body or your well-being. I've been called in to advise at an informal meeting of political and influential figures from around the Pacific Rim. It will last a week. My personal assistant in London is unable to help—he has family problems. I need someone who can type well, find information on a wide variety of subjects, check its accuracy and collate it in time for me to be armed for each session. Someone who's discreet. You'll be busy, but there should be enough time for you to swim and otherwise enjoy yourself. Obviously, you'll be well compensated for your time.'

The lick of irritation underlying his words angered her, but was oddly reassuring. It sounded as though she were merely the easiest solution to an unexpected difficulty. And in Fala'isi it was highly unlikely she'd come up against any situation she couldn't deal with.

However, it was the thought of her bank balance that made the decision. She needed the money. And she wasn't likely to lose either her head or her heart in a week.

'All right, I'll do it,' she said quickly, before she could change her mind. 'But I'll need an address and contact details.'

She'd give them to her landlady. Just in case…

* * *

Three hours later Taryn was sitting in a sleekly luxurious jet feeling as though she'd been tossed without ceremony onto a merry-go-round. Cade had taken over, efficiently organising their departure.

The first shock had been the helicopter ride to the international airport at Auckland. The second arrived hot on its heels when, after swift formalities, Cade escorted her to this plane. The third came when she realised that not only was it private but they were the only passengers.

Feeling ridiculously as though she'd been kidnapped, she obeyed the pilot's instructions and strapped herself in, and they were soon streaking northwards over an ocean as serene as its name. Taryn knew how swiftly the Pacific Ocean could turn violent, but today it was rippling watered silk, agleam all the way to the horizon beneath a sky just as blue and benign.

Not that she could concentrate on it; a few moments ago Cade had finished concisely briefing her on what she'd be expected to do in Fala'isi.

She said warily, 'I assume you won't want me

attending the social occasions.' He'd spoken of cruises, dinners, a cocktail party...

His brows lifted. 'I don't expect you to work for the entire time. If you don't want to attend any of the social occasions that's not a problem. You grew up in the tropics—have you ever been to Fala'isi?'

'No.' She paused, then said lightly, 'But, from what I remember, tropical islands in the Pacific have coconut palms and coconut crabs, and most of them are surrounded by lagoons of the most amazing blue on the planet. There's glorious singing, and whole families somehow manage to perch on little motor scooters.'

'Your parents were brave taking a young child so far from civilisation.'

There was no condemnation in his tone but she had to control a spurt of defensiveness. Her parents didn't need defending. 'They're experienced sailors. And they were desperately needed—still are. There are very few doctors in the outlying islands. My parents are kept busy.'

'So they settled in Aramuhu for your schooling?'

'Yes,' she said briefly.

'Where are they now?' Cade asked, his blue-grey eyes intent.

'Back in the islands,' she told him, wondering a second too late if she should have hedged, let him believe they were within reach. 'In a bigger, more easily sailed yacht that's also a mobile clinic.'

A clinic that the unexpected and very generous donation from Peter had helped to fund. When he'd received the advance for his sculpture, he'd transferred the money into her account.

Horrified, she'd wanted to return it, only to have him grin and say, 'Let me do this, darling girl—it's probably the only time I'm ever going to do anything altruistic. You bring out the best in me.'

He'd had to talk hard to persuade her, but in the end she'd accepted it. He'd been pleased when she'd shown him a photograph of the yacht…

Hastily, she glanced away to hide the tears that stung her eyes.

'Do you see them often?' Cade asked.

'No.' Something in his expression made her say crisply, 'I suppose that sounds as though I don't get on with them but I do—and I admire them tremendously for what they're doing. I think I told you I'd been overseas for two years, having a ball in London and working there to finance trips to the Continent.' She added with a smile, 'Known to all young Kiwis as the big OE—overseas experience. It's a rite of passage.'

Cade leaned back in the seat and took a swift glance at her profile. 'When did your parents go back to the Pacific islands on their mission of mercy?' he asked, keeping his voice detached.

'Once I'd settled at university,' she said cheerfully. 'And now I've revealed some of my story, how about yours?'

Ironically amused, he met coolly challenging green-gold eyes, their size and colour emphasised by dark lashes and brows. No way was he going to tell her of his early childhood; he'd padlocked those memories and thrown away the key years ago.

Cade wondered if she realised just how much she'd revealed. *Admire* didn't mean the same as love. It sounded as though her parents had seen her through school and then more or less abandoned her.

And he was beginning to believe she didn't know that he and Peter had been brothers. If she did, she'd have been a little more wary when she'd spoken of her time in London.

He said economically, 'My life? Very standard. Good parents, good education, a university scholarship, first job in the City, then striking out on my own.'

'And then success,' she supplied with a smile.

Cade caught the hint of satire in the curve of her mouth.

Yes, she was challenging him, and not just sexually, although he was extremely aware of her in the seat beside him. His body stirred at the recollection of the silky texture of her skin and the smooth curves her bikini had displayed.

'That too,' he said non-committally. 'Does success interest you?'

She considered the question, her forehead wrinkling. To his surprise, he realised he was waiting for her answer with some expectation. Which was reasonable; he'd hired her to remove her from her comfort zone so he could find out what sort of person she really was.

Of course, he wouldn't allow himself to be distracted—he didn't do distraction. Not even when it came as superbly packaged as Taryn Angove.

'It interests everyone, surely,' she said at last. 'But it depends on how you define it. My parents are hugely successful because they're doing exactly what they want to do, which is helping people—making a difference to their lives. Sometimes *saving* their lives.'

'So that's your definition? Success means following your passion?'

She gave him a startled look, then laughed, a sound without much humour. 'Seems to be.'

Something more than idle curiosity persuaded him to ask, 'Do you have a passion?'

He saw her withdrawal, but she answered with a rueful smile, 'Not one I've discovered yet. What's your definition of success?'

That had changed over the years, from his initial instinctive need to survive a neglectful, drug-addicted mother. He had no intention of divulging his motivations to anyone, let alone Taryn, who'd made out a list that ended in *disengage from Jason*.

The list had been on the table, as though she'd dropped it there when he'd arrived to pick her up a few hours ago. She'd gone into her bedroom to bring out her pack, and deliberately and without guilt he'd read down the items. He needed all the ammunition he could muster to remind him that her reaction to Peter's proposal had so shattered his brother he'd killed himself.

When had she added that last significant note? After they'd met yesterday?

Jason presumably had been her lover; the journalist had certainly bristled with a territorial air when he'd been talking to her.

So she hadn't mourned Peter for long.

CHAPTER FOUR

THAT thought grated so much Cade turned his head and looked out at the sea below.

One thing the years with an erratic mother had taught him was to read people. As soon as he'd met Taryn he'd noted the subtle signs of her response to him. What he hadn't anticipated was his own reaction to her—a quick, fierce hunger he was having difficulty controlling.

But what worried him was an unexpected and alarmingly unwelcome inclination to believe every word she said. Cade was cynical rather than suspicious, but his life and career had taught him not to trust anyone until he knew them.

And that, he reminded himself, was why Taryn was sitting beside him—in order for him to gather information about her.

He said, 'I suppose my definition of my own

success is to do whatever I do well. And to keep faith with the people who rely on me.'

She waited as though expecting more, then nodded, her expression thoughtful. 'Sounds good.'

And meant very little, she thought a touch sardonically. If she'd hoped to get something other than platitudes from him, she'd just learned he wasn't going to open up to her.

After all, he was now her employer. There were protocols to be observed, a suitably respectful distance to be kept. Possibly, in a subtle English way, he was indicating she'd better forget the informal, unconventional circumstances in which they'd met.

Glancing up, she met hooded steel-blue eyes, unsparing and probing. Sensation sizzled through her and she said the first thing that came to mind. 'I hope I can do the job.'

In an indifferent voice, he said, 'Having second thoughts, Taryn?'

When she shook her head he went on, 'Fala'isi is a civilised place, and all I expect from you is a week of quite straightforward work.' His voice hardened. 'Because you are beautiful there will be people who misunderstand our relationship, but I'm sure you're sophisticated enough to deal with that.'

Heat burned across her cheekbones. Cade's tone had been casually dismissive, as though in his world beauty was taken for granted.

He was far too perceptive. She'd barely recognised the caution in herself, a warning based on nothing more than her own response to him. Time to show him she could be completely professional.

'Of course I can,' she said. She added, 'And I don't suspect you of ulterior motives.'

He nodded. 'Good.' And began to talk of their destination, of the two cultures that had been so successfully integrated by the family that ruled Fala'isi, and of the vibrant economy that made the island state one of the powers in the Pacific.

Taryn listened and commented; from her parents she knew enough about island politics to appreciate the sharp intelligence of his remarks, the astute judgement and skilful manipulation of information. Not that he revealed much of his feelings; he probably felt they were none of her concern.

And he was entirely right; this inchoate desire to understand him was neither comfortable nor sensible.

But he did say, 'It's more than possible that somebody might try to pump you for information about me.'

'They'll fail,' she said promptly, 'because I don't know anything about you.'

He raised his eyebrows. 'You didn't research me on the Internet?'

'Yes, of course.' As far as she'd been able. She'd downloaded a couple of pictures of him with stunning women, and read several articles about his business tactics, but she'd found nothing personal about him. 'Just as anyone else could.'

He showed his teeth in a mirthless smile. 'I'm sure I don't need to tell you to be discreet.'

'No,' she said shortly.

'Good.' He looked up as the cabin attendant came through.

Taryn welcomed the interruption. She was probably imagining the unspoken undercurrents that swirled beneath the mundane words he'd spoken. Yes, he'd called her beautiful—but in a tone of voice that gave no indication what effect she had on him.

She wrenched her mind away from such a subversive thought. OK, so she was acutely conscious of Cade—and she now knew he liked what he saw when those hard, crystalline eyes roved her face, but she understood how little that superficial appreciation meant.

What would her parents think of the man beside her, at present intent on a sheaf of notes?

Her gaze traced the arrogant lines and angles of his profile, the olive skin and arrogantly perfect line of mouth and chin…

Physically, he was magnificent. And after searching the Internet the previous evening she knew he was renowned for his ferociously brilliant mind and what one commentator called his *iron-bound integrity*. Another had commented on his almost *devilish good luck*.

What were his parents like? She'd found a reference to his *climb from the stifling medioc-*

rity of middle-class England but nothing else personal.

Unless you counted the photographs of him with exquisite women. At the thought of those women—bejewelled, superbly groomed, confident—a foolish pang of envy darkened her mood.

He looked up and for a moment their eyes locked. Her confusion turned into a flash of fire at the base of her spine, in the pit of her stomach.

It was quickly dampened by his drawled question. 'Something bothering you?'

'No,' she said swiftly and not, he suspected, entirely truthfully.

He was convinced of it when she added, 'I was wondering if you have a Mediterranean heritage.'

Cade shrugged negligently. 'Not that I'm aware of.'

He didn't know who his birth father was—it could have been anyone. His real father, the one who'd loved him and disciplined him and shown him how to be a man, was ruddy of complexion and blue-eyed, but Harold Cooper had handed on far more important things than superficial physical features.

Cade had no illusions as to what his life would have been if he hadn't been fostered by the Coopers.

He'd have grown up on the streets and probably ended up in jail, possibly dying young like his wretched mother before him. Instead, he'd been loved and cared for, given rules to live by, taught everything he needed to make a success of his life.

Even when his new parents had had their miracle—the child they'd been told would never eventuate—their love for Cade had never faltered. Peter had been a joy to them all, a beloved small brother for Cade to protect and help.

He owed the Coopers everything but the fact of being born—and he was prepared to do anything to give his mother the closure she craved.

Why had Peter chosen to end his life? It had to be something to do with Taryn.

Cade was accustomed to finding answers, and he needed this answer more than any other. His mother feared that Peter had died because he hadn't felt valued by his parents.

The Coopers had certainly been worried about Peter's choice of career, but he had real artistic talent and, once they'd realised he was determined to make his own path, they'd stopped suggesting he choose something steady and reliable.

One way or another, Cade would get to the truth. It shouldn't take him long to discover Taryn's weaknesses and use them to find out what he needed to know.

He glanced across; she'd picked up a magazine and was skimming the pages, stopping now and then to read more carefully. She was beautiful in a healthy, girl-next-door kind of way, her clear green-gold eyes seeming to hide no secrets; her attitude was candid and direct. Cade could see nothing in her to suggest she'd mock a man's offer of love.

Yet she must have cut Peter's confidence to shreds for him to choose death rather than face life without her.

Into Cade's mind came that final note on the list she'd made out: *disengage from Jason*.

Had she *disengaged* from Peter too, then gone on to view the world with that same innocent gaze?

It would be interesting, he thought grimly, to see Taryn's reaction when she found out the accommodation waiting for them on Fala'isi. She knew he was rich; she'd sensed he was attracted to her.

How would she accept sharing the same luxurious beachfront lodgings with him?

Would she see it as an opportunity? With cold self-derision, he fought the kick of desire in his groin and forced his attention back to the papers in his hand.

Taryn looked around the room, furnished in tropical style with lush green plants cooling the flower-scented air. One wall was highlighted by a magnificent *tapa* cloth in shades of tan and cream, black and cinnamon, and in a corner a serene, smoothly sculpted figure of a frigate bird in flight seemed to hover above its pedestal.

Peter would have loved it…

The knot of apprehension in her stomach

loosened when Cade said, 'Choose whichever bedroom you'd like.'

Helpfully, the porter said, 'That room over there has a very beautiful view of the lagoon, madam, and the one on the other side of the *fale* has a lovely intimate view of the pool and the terrace garden.'

She looked at Cade.

Shrugging, he said in a tone that edged on curtness, 'I don't mind where I sleep.'

Taryn responded equally crisply, 'In that case, I'll take the one with the pool view.'

The porter, tall and magisterial, smiled his approval as he scooped her very downmarket pack from the trolley and headed towards the bedroom.

Shoulders held stiffly, Taryn followed him. She'd not expected to be whisked by luxury launch from the airport on the main island of Fala'isi to a fairy tale atoll twenty minutes offshore, nor to be ushered into a beachfront bungalow she was expected to share with Cade Peredur.

That was when she'd faltered, only to feel foolish when Cade said, 'There are two bedrooms.'

'Each with its own bathroom, madam,' the porter had supplied in a reassuring voice that made her even more self-conscious.

OK, so for a moment—but only a moment—she *had* wondered if she'd walked into a situation she didn't even want to think about. But there was no need for the glint of satirical amusement in Cade's hard eyes. She was not an overwrought idiot, seeing danger where there was none!

After a quick survey of the room she'd chosen, she smiled at the porter when he set her pack tenderly onto the luggage rack.

'Thank you, this is perfect,' she said.

'The lagoon is excellent to swim in, madam,' the porter told her before ushering her into the bathroom, where he demonstrated the switches that lowered the blinds and showed her how to work the multitude of jets in the shower.

The bathroom was circular, its walls built of rock topped by a glass ceiling that allowed a view of palm fronds against a sky of such intense blue it made her blink.

The porter noted the direction of her gaze. 'The

rocks are from the main island—from a lava flow of ancient times.'

His warmth and innate dignity brought back childhood memories and lifted her heart. If it weren't for her unusual response to the man in the next room, she'd relish this return to the tropics.

But without Cade Peredur she wouldn't be here.

She did her best to repress an excitement she hadn't allowed herself to feel for years—since the debacle of her engagement to Antony. Since then, any time she'd felt an emotional rapport, she'd reminded herself that men wanted more than affection. For them—for most people—love included passion.

She'd been utterly convinced she loved Antony, and just as certain that the stirrings of sexual attraction would progress to desire.

Her mouth twisting into a painful grimace, she turned and walked back into the bedroom, thanking the porter as he left.

She'd been so wrong. Making love with Antony had been a disaster. Try as hard as she could, she'd been unable to respond. In the end, her frigidity had caused their love to wither and die in pain and bitter acrimony.

Which was why she'd been so relieved when Peter had shown no signs of wanting anything more than friendship...

And dwelling on a past she couldn't change was fruitless and energy-sapping.

Although this exclusive, secluded retreat had probably been built with extremely wealthy honeymooners in mind, this was a business situation. If she kept that in mind and stayed utterly, coolly professional, she'd enjoy her stay in Fala'isi.

She allowed herself a single wistful glance at the aquamarine pool before unpacking her meagre allowance of clothes and indulging in a quick refreshing shower. For a few seconds she dithered, trying to decide on the most suitable garment.

Which was silly. As part of the office furniture, no one would notice what she wore. Firming her mouth, she slipped on a pair of cool, floaty trousers and a soft green shirt, combed her hair into a smooth cap and tied it back, then re-applied her only lipstick and after a deep breath walked back into the big, airy living room.

Her treacherous heart bumped at the sight of Cade, tall and dark in casual clothes, standing on the terrace. He turned before she'd taken more than a couple of steps into the room and watched her come through the huge glass doors to join him.

That cool scrutiny set every nerve twanging with eager, anticipatory, thoroughly scary awareness.

'Everything all right?' he asked.

'Absolutely.' She tore her gaze away to examine the surroundings. 'Whoever set this place up certainly homed into the romantic ambience of the South Seas.'

Palms shaded the bamboo furniture, luxuriously upholstered in white. Impressive boulders—probably also relics of the fiery creation of the main island—skilfully contrasted with vast earthenware pots holding lushly foliaged shrubs and, a few steps away, thick white rope provided the hand-rail in the shimmering pool. Bold, brilliant flowers danced in the sun, their colours clashing with a sensuous bravura Taryn envied.

'The Chapmans—the family who rule Fala'isi—are famous for their acumen and their commitment to excellence,' Cade said coolly. 'They know what people expect from a place like this.'

'They're also noted for steering Fala'isi so well the islanders now have the highest standard of living in the Pacific Islands. And that,' Taryn finished, 'is much more important.'

He gave another of those piercing looks, as though she'd startled him, and then to her surprise he nodded. 'I agree.'

So he wasn't as cynical and arrogant as she'd suspected.

He resumed, 'We'll eat lunch here, and then I have some facts I'd like you to check and validate while I attend a preliminary meeting. It shouldn't take much more than an hour, so once you've finished I suggest you do some exploring, swim if you want to.'

'On my own?' she couldn't help saying.

His short laugh acknowledged the hit. 'It would be extremely bad for business to allow anyone to drown here.'

'Does that mean there's always someone keeping watch?'

'Discreetly,' he said, a sardonic note sharpening

the word. He surveyed her face and said with the perception she was beginning to expect from him, 'You don't like that.'

'Not particularly.'

He didn't say *Get used to it*, but that was probably what he was thinking. Thankful she didn't live in his world, she added, 'But that won't stop me swimming.'

And wished she'd stayed silent when she recognised a note of defiance in her tone.

'Somehow I didn't expect it to. You seem to live life on your own terms.'

For some reason, his comment startled her. 'Doesn't everyone?'

'You're remarkably innocent if you believe that,' he said cynically. 'Most people meekly follow society's dictates all their life. They buy what they're told to buy, live where they're told to live, in some societies even marry whoever they're told to marry. You appear to be a free spirit.'

'I don't think there's any such thing as true freedom,' she said slowly, then stopped.

She did not want to open herself up to Cade Peredur. It would be safer to establish boundaries, a definite distance between them, because instinct told her that even this sort of fragile, getting-to-know-you exploration could be dangerous.

There's that word again...

She laughed and finished brightly, 'And I've never thought of myself as a free spirit. It sounds great fun.'

And braced herself for another sceptical Peredur scrutiny.

Instead, he picked up a sheaf of papers. 'Around five I might have notes for you to transcribe—not many, as this afternoon's meeting is a procedural one. At seven we'll head off to pre-dinner drinks, and dinner will be at eight.'

Startled, she stared at him. 'What do you mean—*we*? You told me I wouldn't be expected to go to any of the social occasions.'

'That was because I hadn't realised most of the men were bringing their wives and significant others.' He stemmed her impetuous protest with an upheld hand. 'Don't bother pointing out that you're neither. I've just been down that road with Fleur Chapman, the wife of the man who's convened this conference. She wouldn't hear of you being left out.'

Colour stung her cheekbones. Of course he would have objected; social occasions were not in this job description. 'I'm here as your researcher, not to attend parties.'

He responded just as crisply, 'Mrs Chapman has heard of your parents' work, and can see no reason why you shouldn't attend. In fact, she was appalled to think of you staying hidden in the *fale* like a shameful secret, as she put it.'

Dismayed, Taryn stared at him. He—and Mrs Chapman—had cut the ground from under her feet, and she suspected he knew it. Possibly he resented being forced to take her with him.

No more than she did, but the Chapman family had ruled Fala'isi for a couple of centuries; not only were they extremely rich, they were a powerful force in the Pacific where their descent from the ancient chiefly family of Fala'isi gave them huge prestige.

If the Chapmans were interested in her parents' work, she thought suddenly, there was a chance they might be prepared to help. With so many worthwhile calls on charity spending, her mother and father scrabbled for enough money to keep their clinics going.

This was possibly something she could do for her parents.

But she made one further effort. 'I haven't brought any suitable clothes.'

Dispassionately, Cade said, 'Naturally I'll organise that.' Overriding her instant horrified objection, he went on, 'The manageress of the boutique here will be along about three to discuss what you'll need.'

'I can't let you pay for my clothes,' she blurted.

One straight black brow lifted. 'You can't stop me,' he observed with cool amusement. 'Whether or not you wear them is entirely up to you.'

The prospect of appearing in public with him—in clothes he had paid for—sent prickles of apprehension across her skin. There would be sideways glances and assumptions, some of them almost certainly salacious, and the sort of gossip she despised.

Apparently he could read her mind, because he

startled her anew by saying in a hard voice, 'If anyone—anyone at all—says anything untoward, I'll deal with it.'

Of course he wasn't being protective, she thought, alarmed by the swift rush of warmth his words caused. She quelled it by telling herself that he wouldn't want them to be connected in any way.

Office girl and tycoon? Not with the lovely Lady Someone in his life.

Stoutly, she responded, 'I'm quite capable of looking after myself, thank you.'

Anyway, she doubted if anyone would mistake her for Cade's latest lover; no matter what she wore, she couldn't achieve that elegant, exclusive, expensive look.

'I've noticed,' he said dryly, 'but in this case you won't need to.'

When she looked up he was smiling. Her heart flipped, honing her awareness into something so keen and compelling she felt it in her bones. Tension pulled through her, strong as a steel hawser, and it took all her will not to take a step towards him.

She managed to resist, but couldn't conquer the reckless impulse to smile back at him, although her voice was uneven when she said, 'How often does someone tell you you're a very dictatorial man?'

Involuntarily, Cade responded to her smile; it was pure challenge backed by a hint of invitation, and he guessed she was trying to force a reaction from him, judge for herself why he'd brought her here.

It took an exercise of will to clear the urgent hunger that fogged his brain.

OK, he wanted her—but, much more than that, he wanted what she knew. Instead of confronting her directly about Peter's death, he'd decided on a more subtle approach—one that did *not* involve acting on this elemental attraction, as unwanted as it was powerful.

However, he couldn't stop himself from saying, 'Calling me dictatorial makes me sound like some blood-thirsty despot intent on holding on to power by any means, no matter how cruel. How often does someone tell you you're beautiful and ask you why you're still unattached?'

Her eyes widened, then were veiled by thick, dark lashes. 'Rarely,' she said curtly. 'And usually it's as a sleazy pick-up line from a man I wouldn't be seen dead with.'

'Touché.' OK, so he'd been blunt, but what the hell had caused the frozen shock he'd seen for a millisecond before her expression had closed him out?

Something shattering. Peter's suicide? Possibly.

Damn, he thought, as sounds from outside heralded the arrival of waiters with lunch. *Damn and double damn*. Their inopportune arrival might have cut off a chance to introduce the subject.

He was going to have to, sooner or later, yet he found himself intensely disinclined to raise the matter. And that was a worry.

'Ah, here's lunch,' he said, his voice as clipped and curt as he could make it.

It was impossible to tell what she was thinking, but she responded calmly, 'Good, I'm hungry. And I'm really looking forward to diving into the lagoon. It's too long since I swam in really warm water.'

Into his head flashed a tantalising image of her in her bikini, all slender limbs and silken skin, a gleaming, golden nymph from one of the raunchier legends.

Angered by the violent involuntary response from his body, Cade headed for his own room, but stopped at the door to say over his shoulder, 'When you do swim, make sure you use sunscreen.'

'Yes, sir,' she responded smartly. 'New Zealand spends summer under a huge hole in the ozone layer, and wearing hats and slapping on sunscreen at frequent intervals has become part of our national character.'

Cade had to hide a smile. Over lunch, served on the terrace, he asked her about her childhood and, although she spoke readily enough about that, she was surprisingly reticent about other aspects of her life. He already knew she'd been engaged once, but when he'd provided her with an opportunity to mention it, she hadn't.

Which proved nothing, he thought, irritated by a potent mixture of feelings—the sensual hunger somehow magnified by a growing protectiveness.

Clearly she didn't feel her parents had abandoned her. In fact, she'd snapped at the bait he'd dangled in front of her by mentioning that Fleur Chapman might be able to help them in their mission of mercy.

So the fact that they'd more or less left her to her own devices once she'd left secondary school didn't seem to concern her. He felt an odd sympathy, remembering his own parents' sacrifices— the money saved for a trip to France, the gap year they'd insisted on financing…

During the afternoon meeting he found it surprisingly hard to concentrate; his mind kept slipping back to the smooth fall of Taryn's hair, turned by the sun into a flood of burnished copper, the way her crisp voice was softened by an intriguing husky undertone, her open pleasure in the food.

And that, he thought grimly as he headed back to their *fale*, was something new; no other woman had come between him and work. He'd liked his lovers, enjoyed spending time with them—even Louisa, before she'd decided to change the rules of their relationship. But his previous women had only occupied a small niche in his life.

Taryn Angove was different. How different? He searched for a word to describe her, and could only come up with fresh—*fresh* and apparently frank, intensely seductive.

Had Peter too thought she was different?

Cade welcomed the acid bite of that thought; it dragged his mind back to focus. He couldn't afford to let his hormones overpower his brain cells.

A call on his cell phone interrupted him; he stopped beneath a large spreading tree with brazen scarlet flowers and spoke to the private detective who'd been investigating Taryn.

When the call was over he pocketed the cell phone and punched one hand into the palm of his other. Beneath his breath, he said explosively, 'Why the hell did you have to do it, Peter? Why didn't you just laugh straight back in her face and find a woman who could love you? Why take the coward's way out?'

The bitter words shocked him into silence. He lifted his gaze to the sea, but saw Taryn walking across the sand towards the *fale*, the *pareu* slung across her hips emphasising their seductive sway.

Water turned her hair into gleaming copper and gilded her skin so that she seemed to walk in a golden, shimmering aura. She was even more alluring than the images his brain had been conjuring all afternoon.

Heated desire gripped him so fiercely he had to turn away. It would be no hardship to seduce her, he thought grimly, no hardship at all.

Yet he could not. Dared not. Never before had hunger fogged his brain, whispering a temptation he wanted to yield to.

CHAPTER FIVE

CADE dragged his gaze away from Taryn, trying to clear his mind by fixing his attention on the hibiscus bush a few feet away. The fiercely magenta heart of each flower glowed in a silken gold ruff, hues so intense he was reminded of the time he'd visited an official mint and watched molten gold being poured.

Taryn had a quick, astute brain and plenty of character, so she was unlikely to be drifting without purpose. Yet since she'd got back from England her only job had been selling souvenirs to summer tourists, and she certainly didn't seem to be in a hurry to find more work.

He found himself strongly resisting what should have been the obvious reason. If she had most of Peter's advance in her bank account, she wouldn't need to worry about working for some years.

Everything pointed to her being the one who'd

accepted—or stolen—the money from his brother. There was no proof, yet no other person had been close enough to Peter to make it seem likely he'd have given them money. If he'd showered her with it, only to have his proposal turned down with mockery and laughter, then that could have been a reason for Peter's tragic decision.

And she hadn't mentioned Peter. Or shown any signs of grief.

An innate sense of justice forced him to admit he didn't expect her to break into sobs every half hour. That wouldn't be her style.

Nor his, yet he grieved deeply for his brother.

So, was she as good as he was at hiding her feelings—or did she have none? His eyes narrowing, he watched her stop at the outdoor shower set under a big poinciana tree. She tossed the length of fabric around her hips over a shrub, turned on the tap and lifted her face to let the water flow over her.

The bikini was decorous enough but, moulded against the clean curves of her body by the veil of water, she might as well have been naked.

Was this a deliberate pose, letting him see what she had on offer?

Lust tugged urgently at him, swamping his cold calculation with a hot, angry hunger. Abruptly, he turned away, overcome with self-disgust. He couldn't let himself become too fixated on her. He'd always been in charge of his physical reactions; it was humiliating to want a woman who might be everything he despised.

He had to persuade her to open up so he could better judge whether to trust her version of what had happened. He needed to see for himself what she'd felt—if anything—for his brother.

Mouth set in a firm line, he headed down the shell path to the *fale*.

Taryn almost hummed with pleasure beneath the shower, but water was likely to be precious on a coral atoll, so she turned off the tap and wrapped her *pareu* around her again to mop up.

She was so glad to be back in the tropics. Stroking through the silken waters of the lagoon, she'd felt a surge of something very close to renewal. Oh, the warm sea against her skin, the sand shimmering white against the green bushes beneath the coconut palms—they all had something to do with it but, although the sun beat down with a languorous intensity only known in the tropics, her raised spirits were caused by something deeper than delight at being back, a feeling much stronger, much more intimate than a sensory lift, welcome though that was.

It was strangely like a rebirth, an understanding that life could be worthwhile again.

And it had *nothing*—not a thing—to do with being here with Cade, whose controlled dynamism was a force to be reckoned with. Perhaps she'd finally accepted that she'd never know why Peter had changed so abruptly from a best friend to a would-be husband...

Or whether her shocked refusal had led to his suicide.

Her bitter remorse at her stunned response would always be with her. But from somewhere she'd found a renewed sensation of confidence, of control of her own destiny.

Once she got back to New Zealand she'd find a job—move to Auckland if it was necessary—and start this next stage of her life.

There was no sign of Cade when she reached their accommodation. Squelching a stupid disappointment she walked through the glass doors into her bedroom, bare feet warm against the cool smooth tiles on the floor.

Perhaps she could put her skills as a librarian to use in some tropical area?

She smiled ironically. If she managed to find such a position she wouldn't be living in a place like this, subtly groomed and organised to give rich, demanding clients the illusion of paradise.

Strange that here, in a spot dedicated to a romantic idea of leisure and sensuous relaxation, she should feel a resurgence of the energy she'd lost when Peter died.

She was dressed and combing her wet hair back from her face when movement caught her eye. Swivelling, she realised that Cade had walked to the edge of the terrace and was bending to pick a hibiscus flower.

For some peculiar reason, her heart lurched at the sight of his long fingers stroking the ruffled, satiny petals—only to freeze a moment later when a casual, dismissive flick of his fingers sent the exquisite bloom onto the ground.

It shouldn't have affected her so strongly. Yet she almost gasped with shock, and took an instinctive step sideways to hide from sight.

After a few seconds she told herself she was being ridiculous. She forced herself to breathe again and glanced sideways into an empty garden. Her heartbeat settling into its usual steady rhythm, she scolded herself for being so foolishly sensitive. Nothing had happened. He'd merely picked a flower and tossed it away.

Later, when she emerged from her room, Cade was standing just outside the glass doors with his back to her. He had to have excellent hearing because, although she moved quietly, he turned the moment she came into the big, cool living room.

Their eyes met, and another little chill ran the length of her spine until he smiled. 'Enjoy your swim?' he asked.

'It was lovely,' she said, oddly disconcerted. Had he seen her walk up from the beach? She repressed a sensuous little shiver. She'd been perfectly decent with her *pareu* draped around her—and he was probably bored by the sight of women parading around in bikinis.

'How did you find the computer set-up?'

She blinked, then hastily reassembled her wits. 'Oh, excellent. No problems.'

He nodded. Now, he thought stringently— give her that opportunity now. Yet it took all his notorious drive to say casually, 'Your computer skills would have come in handy when you were in London.'

Taryn smiled. 'Not at first. I worked in a coffee shop, until a friend found me a job cataloguing a library, which was perfect. I could dash over the Channel or around the country whenever I wanted, providing I got the work done.'

'A very good friend,' Cade observed. 'One who knew you well.'

'Yes, a good friend indeed,' she said tone- lessly.

Cade sent a keen glance, but could read nothing from her smooth face. He let the silence drag on but all she did was nod.

Cade held out a sheaf of notes. 'I'd like you to get these down now.'

Heart thudding, Taryn took the notes and escaped into her room. It was a relief to sit down at the desk and concentrate on the swift, bold handwriting, and an even greater relief when he left to meet someone.

When she'd finished getting his clear, concise notes into the computer and backed them up, she closed things down and stood up. Cade had just returned and the sun was heading towards the horizon. It would seem to fall more quickly as it got closer to the clear, straight line where sea met sky, and there might be a mysterious green flash the instant it slipped over the horizon. She'd seen it a couple of times, and looked forward to seeing it again.

She picked up the printed copy and walked into the sitting room. Cade got up from the sofa where he'd been reading the work she'd collated after lunch.

After a quick perusal of the copy, he said, 'This is exactly what I need, thank you.' He glanced at his watch. 'You have half an hour to get into whatever you're wearing to cocktails and dinner.'

When she frowned, he said smoothly, 'I assume you've chosen something suitable to wear.'

Under the boutique manager's interested survey she'd chosen something, but whether it was suitable or not time would tell. Impulsively, she said, 'It still seems too much like gatecrashing for me to feel comfortable about going.'

'We've already had this conversation. You've been personally invited.' His mouth curled up at the corners. 'Of course, if you met someone on the beach you'd like to further your acquaintance with—'

'No,' she interrupted, startled.

'Then what's your problem?'

Taryn hesitated. Impossible to tell him that for some reason she hated the thought of being tagged as just another of his women, a holiday convenience.

But his cool, speculative gaze demanded an answer. Gathering her wits, she snapped, 'I'm your researcher, not arm candy.'

His smile stopped any further words, a smile

that, allied to such a powerful presence, made him a walking, breathing, potently dangerous adrenalin rush.

'Candy is sweet. Your tongue is far too sharp for you to be considered anything like that.' He took her hand. 'If you don't get going we'll be late.'

It was like brushing against an electric fence, she thought wildly. Breathing was impossible. Dumbfounded by the wildfire intensity of her re-action to his touch, she let him turn her towards her room.

'Off you go,' he said calmly, and started her off with a movement so gentle it could hardly be called a push.

Taryn's body responded automatically and she got halfway to her room before her dazzled brain came to life. How dared he? Frowning, she swung around and, in her most forthright voice, said, 'I'm not a child to be told to go to my room. And please don't ever push me like that again.'

His brows climbed. 'I'm sorry,' he said unex-pectedly, adding abruptly, 'And you don't need to be afraid of me. I don't hurt women.'

The words burst out before she could stop them. 'I'm not afraid of you!'

Cool it! She was overreacting, giving too much away, allowing him to see how strongly he affected her. After a jagged breath, she said crossly, 'I just hate it when people stop a perfectly good rant by apologising.'

That spellbinding smile made a brief reappearance. 'I take your point, but you haven't time for a really good rant right now. Later, you can let go all you like.'

An equivocal note in his voice dried her throat. She could read nothing in the starkly handsome face, and surely he wasn't hinting...

He resumed, 'You flinched when I touched you.'

Wishing she'd ignored it, she said, 'Not because I was afraid. I just wasn't expecting it. And, although I'm delighted you don't hurt women, how are you with children and animals?'

He subjected her to a look she could barely parry. Silkily, he said, 'Superb.' She was choking back laughter when he added, 'And, to reassure you, from now on I'll only touch you after asking permission.'

His smile, and the glinting look that accompanied it, stopped her breath again. He *was* flirting with her!

Common sense warned her she was way out of her league—but there was no reason to let him know that.

Rallying, she said, 'So you'll say, "Taryn, I want to push you out of the way of that shark. Is that all right?" And then wait for my answer?'

'If that happens, I might force myself to ignore this conversation,' he said smoothly.

A note in his voice produced a swift wave of heat across her cheekbones. This was dangerous stuff. Put an end to it right now, she commanded herself.

But how?

OK, she'd pretend to take him seriously, as though his eyes weren't gleaming with amusement and her blood wasn't pumping a suspicious and inconvenient excitement through her veins.

In her most prosaic tone, she said, 'Well, that's all right then.' She glanced at her watch as if checking the time. 'And if I'm to be ready on time I'd better get going.'

And managed to force her suddenly heavy legs to move away from him. *Cold shower* was her first thought once she reached the sanctuary of her room.

Icy water would have been good, but she had to content herself with a brisk splash in the luke-warm water available. However, by the time she'd knotted a sleek *pareu* that fell from her bare shoulders to her ankles in a smooth column of gold, her pulse had calmed down—almost.

After a careful examination in the mirror, she gave a short nod of satisfaction. The inexpensive *pareu* looked almost as good as the designer clothes the shop manageress had brought to show her. Her own slim gold sandals made no concession to her height; she could wear ten-centimetre heels and still be shorter then Cade.

Exactly twenty-five minutes after she'd left, she walked back into the sitting room, to meet a narrow-eyed glance from Cade that sent her pulse rate soaring again. In tropical evening clothes, he was *stunning*, she decided faintly, trying to control the overheated reactions ricocheting through her.

His quizzical expression made her realise she was staring a little too openly. Without censoring the thought, she said, 'I hope this is suitable.'

'I'm not an expert on women's clothes,' he said, his level voice mocking her turmoil, 'but no man in the place is going to think it other than perfect.'

She pulled a face. 'It's not the men I'm worried about.'

Hard mouth easing into an oblique smile, he said, 'The women will be envious. You look fine.' A little impatiently, he finished, 'Let's go.'

Nerves tightened in the pit of her stomach as they walked down a shell path beneath the coconut palms to the venue for the cocktail party, a wide terrace open to the sea and the sunset.

Taryn's swift glance told her that every other woman there was clad in designer resort wear, the sort of clothes featured in very upmarket magazines as ideal for the captain's cocktail party.

And, judging by the massed array of jewels sparkling in the light of the westering sun, she was the only employee. Worse, a man who turned to watch them walk in smiled sardonically and said something in a low voice to his companion, an elegant blonde who moved so she could see them both clearly.

Taryn gave them a coolly dismissive glance, tensing when Cade slid a firm hand beneath her elbow.

'Ignore them,' he said in a low, inflexible voice, looking over her at the couple.

Taryn didn't see his expression, but the glance he sent towards them must have been truly intimidating. Their rapid about-face almost amused her, and helped to ease her chagrin.

He commanded, 'Relax.'

Ignoring the rush of heat to her cheeks, she blurted the first thing that came to mind. 'You were going to ask before you touched me again.'

'I did make an exception for sharks,' he said soberly.

She spluttered, then laughed, and he released her. Feeling an abrupt chill, almost as though she'd been abandoned, she took a quick look around, turning as a handsome couple came up to them, their hosts Luke and Fleur Chapman.

After introducing them, Cade said, 'Luke's family are rather like feudal overlords here.' Then he added, 'But you know this, of course. As well as their strong New Zealand connection, your parents keep you up-to-date with Pacific affairs.'

Taryn said cheerfully, 'Ever since a Kiwi married Luke's father we've considered the Chapmans of Fala'isi to be honorary New Zealanders.' She gave a comradely grin to Fleur Chapman. 'And of course our newspapers and every women's magazine had a field day when another Kiwi married Luke.'

Both their hosts laughed, but Fleur said thankfully, 'They seem to have lost interest in us now we've settled into being a boringly married couple.'

The glance she exchanged with her husband made Taryn catch her breath and feel a sudden pang of something too close to envy. Nothing *boring* in that marriage, she thought.

What would it be like to have such complete trust in the person you loved?

Fleur turned back to Taryn. 'And we've heard of the wonderful work your parents do. Later, when we have time, we must talk more about it.'

Their warmth and friendliness set the tone of the evening. Her tension evaporated, and with Cade at her side she felt oddly protected—and that, she realised, was both ridiculous and more than a little ominous.

About the last thing she needed was a man's protection; she'd been looking after herself quite adequately since she left secondary school.

As she smiled and chatted with people she'd previously seen only on the news, she observed their reactions to Cade. Intrigued, she saw that respect for his formidable achievements was very much to the fore, mixed with a certain wariness.

If anyone else was speculating on the relationship between Cade and her, it didn't show. Most of the women noted her clothes, and an observant few even recognised her *pareu* to be a cheap beach wrap from the boutique.

Only one mentioned it, a charming middle-aged

Frenchwoman who said, 'My dear, how clever of you! You put us all to shame with sheer powerful simplicity!'

The unexpected compliment brought a flush to Taryn's skin, making Madame Murat laugh as she turned to Cade. 'I hope you appreciate her.'

Cade's eyes narrowed slightly, but he favoured her with a smile. 'I do indeed,' he said blandly.

Which left Taryn wondering why she felt as though she'd been observing to some covert skirmish.

'I think our hostess is indicating it's time for dinner,' Cade observed.

Obediently, she turned, only to stop in mid-step. 'Oh,' she breathed. 'Oh, *look*.'

With the suddenness of the tropics, the sun vanished below the horizon in a glory of gold and crimson, allowing the darkness that swept across the sea to make landing in a breath of warm air. Torches around the terrace flared into life, their flames wavering gently in the gardenia-scented breeze, and from the distant reef came the muted thunder of eternal waves meeting the solid coral bulwark that protected the lagoon.

'Sometimes there's a green flash,' she said quietly, eyes still fixed on the horizon.

For the first time since Peter's death, Taryn felt a pang of joy, a moment of such pure piercing delight she shivered.

'Are you cold?' Cade murmured. 'Do you need a wrap?'

Taryn couldn't tell him what had happened. Not only was the exaltation too intimate, but in a subversive way Cade's presence had contributed to it, making him important to her in a way beyond the solely physical.

And that was scary. Magnetic and disturbing, yet underpinned by a solidity she found enormously sustaining, Cade was getting too close.

'I'm not cold,' she told him with a return to her usual crispness, 'but somehow I got the idea that the cocktail party and the dinner were two separate events. I'd planned to collect a wrap from the *fale* to wear to dinner.'

'My mistake,' he said blandly. He nodded at a waiter, who came across immediately. Cade said, 'Describe the wrap.'

'It's draped over the end of my bed,' she said,

touched by his thoughtfulness. 'A darker gold than this—bronze, really—with a little bit of beadwork around the sleeves.' And when the man had moved off she said, 'Thank you.'

He nodded, but didn't answer as they walked through a door onto another terrace. A long table was arranged exquisitely, candle flames gleaming against silver and crystal and lingering on pale frangipani flowers and greenery.

Foolish resentment gripped Taryn at the sideways glances Cade was receiving from a very beautiful woman in a slinky black sheath that played up her fragile blonde beauty.

Grow up, she told herself. This was ridiculous; she had absolutely no claim on him. OK, so she felt good. That showed she was getting over the shock of Peter's death. Beyond standing beside her at a sensitive moment, Cade had nothing to do with it.

Nothing at all.

CHAPTER SIX

WHEN Cade took her arm again, Taryn was rather proud of the way she managed to restrain her wildfire response to that casual touch. Too proud, because he sensed it. Fortunately, he put it down to nervousness.

'Relax,' he advised crisply. 'These are just people—good, bad or dull. Often all three at different times.' Without pausing, he went on, 'I asked Fleur to seat us side by side so that you wouldn't have two total strangers to talk to.'

In other words, he thought she was a total social novice. Well, when it came to occasions of this rarefied nature, she *was*, she thought ruefully.

He guessed her reaction. 'Normally, I'm sure you're able to hold your own,' he told her.

'How do you do that?' she asked impulsively.

He knew what she meant. *How do you read my mind?*

After a long considering look that curled her toes, he smiled. 'You have a very expressive face.'

Whereas he'd elevated a poker face to an art form.

Before she could answer, he went on, 'I thought you might be jet-lagged.'

'I don't think so, thank you.' Then she tensed again as his lashes drooped. Her breath locked in her throat. She swallowed and added a little too late, 'But it was kind of you.'

His hooded gaze matched his sardonic tone. 'I try.'

The odd little exchange left her with stretched nerves. Fortunately, the waiter arrived with her wrap and handed it to Cade, who held it out for her. She slid her arms into it and wondered if the brush of his fingers against her bare skin was deliberate or an accident.

Whatever, it sent sensuous little thrills through her as she sat down.

She turned to greet her neighbour, a pleasant middle-aged man from Indonesia. Cade's other dinner partner was the blonde woman with the come-hither gaze and, to Taryn's secret—and embarrassing—irritation, she made an immediate play for the attention he seemed quite happy to give her.

Cattily, Taryn decided that if the woman had anything on beneath the clinging black sheath it would have to be made of gossamer. Her moment of delight evaporated and the evening stretched before her like a punishment.

Several hours later, she heaved a silent sigh of relief when the evening came to an end. Goodbyes and thanks were said and, perhaps emboldened by excellent champagne, the woman in the clinging sheath flung her arms around Cade's neck and kissed him. Although he didn't reject her, he turned his cheek so that her lips barely skimmed it and then, in a gesture that seemed to be steadying, held her away from him.

Not a bit embarrassed, she gazed into his eyes and said huskily, 'I'll look forward to talking to you about that proposition tomorrow.'

Taryn struggled to control her shock and the concentrated venom that cut through her. Jealousy was a despicable emotion—one she had no right to feel.

Nevertheless, she had to tighten her lips to keep back an acid comment when she and Cade were walking away.

Coconuts lined the white shell path, their fronds whispering softly above them in the slow, warm breeze. Taryn struggled to ignore the drowsy, scented ambience that had so seduced the original European explorers they'd thought the Pacific islands the next best place to paradise.

Desperate to break a silence that seemed too charged, she said, 'I once read that human life in the islands would have been impossible without coconuts.'

'When you say *the islands*, you mean the Pacific Islands?' Cade queried.

'Well, yes.' Good, a nice safe subject to settle the seething turmoil inside her.

Somehow, seeing another woman kiss Cade had let loose something primitive and urgent in her—a female possessiveness that sliced through the restraint she'd deliberately imposed on herself after the violent end of her engagement.

It needed to be controlled—and fast. After swallowing to ease her dry throat, she said sedately, 'It's convenient shorthand for New Zealanders when we refer to the Polynesian islands.'

'So are coconut palms native to this region?'

Judging by his cool, dry tone, Cade wasn't aware of her feelings. Thank heavens.

'Possibly.' Yes, her voice sounded good—level, a little schoolmistressy. 'No one seems to know where they originated because they populated the tropics on this side of the world well before any humans arrived here. The nuts can germinate and grow after floating for years and thousands of miles.'

When he didn't reply, she looked up in time to see something dark and fast hurtling down towards her. She gave a choked cry and ducked, stumbling as a vigorous push on her shoulder sent her lurching sideways into the slender trunk of the nearest palm.

She grabbed it and clung. Cade too had avoided whatever it was and as she sagged he pulled her upright, supporting her in a hard, close embrace.

Heart thumping, stunned by the speed of his

response, she asked in a muted, raw voice, 'I think...was it a fruit bat?'

He was silent for a few tense seconds. 'It certainly didn't hit the ground, so it was flying.'

'That's what it would be, then.' Her tone wobbled—affected by a wild onrush of adrenalin, she thought feverishly.

And by Cade's warmth, the disturbing masculine power that locked her in his arms...

No!

Yet she didn't move. 'I'd forgotten about them,' she babbled. 'They don't attack, of course—they just scare the wits out of people who aren't used to them.'

She had to fight the flagrant temptation to bury her face in his shoulder and soak up some of the formidable strength and composure from his lean, powerfully muscled body.

Lean, powerfully muscled—and *aroused* body...

As if reacting to the heat that burned through her, he relaxed his grip a little and looked down.

Taryn's mouth dried and her pulse echoed in

her head, drowning out any coherent thought. Sensation ran riot along insistent, pleading nerves.

Mutely, she met the probing lance of his scrutiny, her lashes drooping as the shifting glamour of moonlight played across the angles and planes of his face, so rigid it resembled a mask.

Except for that glittering gaze fixed on her lips.

As though the words were torn from him, Cade said roughly, 'Damn. This is too soon.'

Taryn froze, every instinct shrieking that this was a bad, foolish, hair-raisingly terrifying statement.

Every instinct save one—the primal, irresistible conviction that if Cade didn't kiss her she'd regret it for ever.

Her lips parted. 'Yes,' she said in a husky, faraway voice. 'Too soon.'

'And you're afraid of me.'

She dragged in a deep breath. Oh, no, not afraid of Cade.

Afraid—*terrified*—of being shown once more that she was cold, too cold to satisfy a man...

But she didn't feel cold. This had never happened before—this wild excitement that shimmered through her like a green flash at sunset, rare and exquisite, offering some hidden glory she might perhaps reach...

She stared up into narrowed eyes, saw the hard line of his mouth and knew he was going to step back, let her return to her chilly, isolated world. Somehow, without intending to, Cade had breached her defences, challenged that self-imposed loneliness, making her want—no, *long*—to rejoin the real world, where people touched and desired and kissed and made love without barriers.

'No,' she blurted, desperate to convince him. 'Not of you—of myself.'

Frowning, Cade demanded, 'Why?'

She had to tell him, but her voice was low and shamed and bitter when she admitted, 'I'm frigid.'

His brows shot up in an astonishment that strangely warmed her. 'Frigid? I don't believe it. Tonight, I saw you literally stopped in your tracks by a sunset. No one who responds so ardently to sensory experiences could possibly be frigid.'

When he bent his head she stiffened, but he said in a quiet voice, 'Relax. I would never hurt you, and I'm not going to leap on you and drag you into the bushes.'

The image of controlled, disciplined Cade losing his cool so completely summoned a spontaneous gurgle of laughter.

He smiled, and traced the outline of her lips with a hand that shook a little. The shame and fear holding her rigid dissipated a fraction, soothed by the sensuous shiver of delight that almost tentative touch aroused.

His voice deep and quiet, he said, 'There are very few frigid women, didn't you know? It's usually a term imposed by clumsy, carelessly inconsiderate men. Who slapped you with that label?'

When she hesitated, he said swiftly, 'If it's too painful—'

'No,' she said wonderingly, because for the first time ever she thought she might be able to talk about it. In his arms, his heart beating solidly against her, she felt a strong sense of security, almost—incredible though that seemed to her bewildered mind—of peace.

Nevertheless, she had to swallow before she could go on. 'It's just that I was engaged but I wasn't able to respond. It upset my fiancé and in the end it mattered too much.'

She stopped. She didn't tell him—had never been able to tell anyone—of the shattering scene that had ended the engagement.

'So, if you truly are frigid, why are you snuggling against me so comfortably?'

Taryn said huskily, 'I don't know.'

'Do you feel completely safe?'

'Yes,' she said instantly.

'So if I kiss you, you're not going to be scared, because it's only going to be a kiss?'

Her whole body clenched as a wave of yearning swept through her—poignant, powerfully erotic and so intense she shivered with it. 'I'm not afraid,' she said, adding a little bitterly, 'Well, I suppose I am, but it's only of freezing you off.'

He lifted her chin. Eyes holding hers, he said

above the wild fluttering of her heart, 'Well, let's see if that happens.'

And his mouth came down on hers.

Somehow, she had expected an unsubtle, dominant passion, so she was startled at first by his gentle exploration. Yet another part of her welcomed it and her mouth softened under his, her body responding with a languorous lack of resistance, a melting that was bone-deep, cell-deep—*heart*-deep.

As if he'd been waiting for that, he lifted his head. 'All right?'

The taut words told her he was holding himself under intense restraint, every powerful muscle in his big body controlled by a ruthless will.

Taryn could have been scared. Instead, a wave of relief and delight overwhelmed her and she turned her head and said against the hard line of his jaw, 'It's—saying that is getting to be a habit with you. I'm absolutely all right.'

He laughed, deep and quiet, and this time the kiss was everything she'd hoped, a carnal expression of hunger, dangerously stimulating, that sent unexpected shivers rocketing through her in a firestorm of reckless excitement.

He raised his head and slid his hands down to her hips, easing her closer. When he resumed the kiss, her breasts yielded to the solid wall of his chest. He was all muscle, all uncompromising strength, summoning from an unknown source in her an intense, aching anticipation that promised so much.

This time when he lifted his head Taryn's knees buckled and she couldn't hold back a low, sighing purr. Cade held her a little away and surveyed her with such a penetrating stare that she closed her eyes to shield herself.

Instantly, his arms loosened, leaving her chilled and bereft, her breasts aching with unfulfilled desire, her body throbbing with frustration.

He asked, 'Did I hurt—?'

'No,' she broke in, and her tender lips sketched a weak smile. 'Of course you didn't—I'd have punched you in the solar plexus if you had.'

An odd half smile curled his mouth. 'You could have tried,' he said, dropping his arms. 'But I suspect that's enough experimentation for now.'

Disappointment clouded her thoughts. For a moment her mind flashed back to the fragile blonde in her clinging black sheath. 'I'm not a frail little flower, easily bruised,' she said tersely.

Why were they talking when they could be repeating those moments of shattering pleasure?

She parried his unreadable survey with a lift of her brows, only to suffer an odd hitch to her heartbeat when his mouth curled into a smile.

'Far from it,' he said and stepped back, away from her. 'And I think we've proved pretty conclusively that you're not frigid, don't you?'

Taryn banished a forlorn shiver. What had she expected? That he'd sweep her off her feet and prove in the best—the *only* way—that Antony had been completely wrong, and she was more than capable of feeling and responding to passion?

Seduce her, in other words. A hot wave of embarrassment made her turn away. There would have been precious little seduction to it—she'd gone up like a bushfire in his arms.

Cade was a sophisticated man. He'd been far more thoughtful than she'd guessed he could be, but a few *experimental* kisses from her weren't going to mean anything to him. And he was making sure she understood it too.

So it was up to her to seem just as worldly, just as relaxed about her newly discovered sexuality as he clearly was with his. 'I…yes,' she muttered. 'Thank you.'

He'd stayed totally in control, whereas the second he touched her she wouldn't have cared if they'd been in the centre of some huge sports stadium as the sole show for tens of thousands of spectators.

With whole banks of spotlights and television cameras focused on them, she enlarged, hot with humiliation.

Kissing Cade had been mind-blowing—and stupid. Out of the frying pan into the fire…

Her grandmother's domestic saying seemed the perfect way to describe her situation. Desperate to get away, she started to walk off.

Without moving, he asked, 'Did you leave something behind?'

Taryn stopped, cheeks burning, when she realised she'd set off in the wrong direction. If he was smiling she'd…

Well, she didn't know what she'd do, but it would be drastic. Pride stiffened her shoulders and straightened her spine as she turned to face him.

He wasn't smiling.

No emotion showed on the arrogant face—no warmth, nothing but a mild curiosity that chilled her through to her bones.

Just keep it light, casual, everyday. After all, she'd kissed quite a few men in her time.

It took most of her courage and all her will to set off in the right direction and say cheerfully, 'No, and I'm blaming you entirely for scrambling my brains. If you want any respectable work from me, I don't think we should allow that to happen again.'

His expression didn't change as he fell into step with her, but his tone was cynical. 'For some reason, I don't think of respectability when I look at you.'

Taryn had to bite her lip to stop herself from asking what he did think of. He might be the sexiest man she'd ever met, and he certainly kissed like any woman's erotic dream, but he was her employer, for heaven's sake.

Worse than that, she admitted with stringent— and strangely reluctant—honesty, she was far too intrigued by him. Letting Cade's addictive kisses get to her could only lead to heartbreak.

If his lovely blonde neighbour at dinner had shown her anything, it was that there would always be women around him, only too eager to fall into his arms and his bed.

'Well, I am respectable. And we have a professional relationship,' she said stiffly.

'We did.' He paused, and when she remained silent he added, 'I suspect it might just have been converted into something entirely different.'

His cool amusement grated. 'No,' she said firmly.

She'd had little experience when it came to emotional adventures, and she'd never known anything like the response that still seethed through her like the effect of some erotic spell.

Well, she'd just shown she could be as foolish as any eighteen-year-old, but she didn't do sensual escapades.

So, if he still wanted to play games, she'd—what?

The sensible reaction would be to run as if hell-hounds were after her.

'No?' he asked almost negligently.

'You've been very kind and understanding, and I am grateful.' She paused, unable to summon any sensible, calm, sophisticated words. In the end, she decided on a partial truth. 'But, although you helped me discover something about myself I didn't know, I don't expect anything more from you than a resumption of our working relationship.'

Cade glanced down. She wasn't looking at him; against the silver shimmer of the lagoon through the palm trunks her profile was elegant, sensuous—and as determined as the chin that supported it.

Oddly enough, he believed she'd been convinced she was frigid. He'd deduced something of it even before she'd told him; her reactions to his touch had warned him of some emotional trauma. Suppressing an uncivilised desire to track down and punish the man who'd done such a number on her, he wondered if this was why she'd refused Peter.

No, she'd *laughed*… That implied a certain crudity—or cruelty.

She'd rejected Peter in a manner that had left him so completely disillusioned he'd been unable to live with the humiliation.

So was now the time to tell her who he was?

Not yet, Cade decided. There was more to Taryn than he'd thought, and he'd only got just below the surface.

Why was she back-pedalling? She must realise she had no need to whet his appetite; he was still fighting to control a ferocious surge of hunger. In his arms she'd been eager and passionate, her willingness summoning sensations more extreme than anything he'd felt since his untamed adolescence.

But she had every right to remind him of their professional relationship. And he had every right to tempt her into revealing herself more. He stamped down on the stray thought that his desire might be gaining the upper hand.

'Fair enough,' he said, finishing, 'Although I

should warn you that I'm particularly fond of exceeding expectations.'

And waited for her reaction.

CHAPTER SEVEN

TARYN gave him a swift, startled glance, faltered on a half step, recovered lithely and looked away but, beneath the shimmering gold *pareu*, her breasts lifted as though she'd taken a deep breath. The languorous perfume of some tropical flower floated with voluptuous impact through the warm air as they turned off the main path towards their accommodation.

Was she resisting an impulse to take the bait? Cade waited, but when she stayed silent continued with a touch of humour, 'However, as we're back to being professional, here's what's happening tomorrow.'

He gave her the programme, finishing with, 'And the day ends with a dinner cruise on the harbour.'

At her nod, he said blandly, 'To which you are, of course, invited.'

'I've given up protesting,' she said, irony colouring the words.

Cade permitted himself a narrow smile as he opened the door. 'And of course you'll be perfectly safe with all those people around.'

'I'm perfectly safe anyway,' she returned a little sharply, and said a rapid, 'Goodnight,' before striding gracefully towards the door of her room.

The fine material of her *pareu* stroked sinuously across the elegant contours of the body beneath it, and he found himself wondering how she would look when it came off...

He waited until she reached for the handle before saying, 'I've always believed that the best strategy was standing and fighting, but retreat is probably the right tactic for you now. Sleep well.'

She turned her head and sent him a long, unwavering look before saying, 'I shall,' and walking through the door, closing it quietly but with a definite click behind her.

Safe behind it, Taryn dragged air into famished lungs and headed for the bathroom, churning with such a complex mixture of emotions she felt as though someone had pushed her head first into a washing machine.

A shower refreshed her marginally, but sleep proved elusive.

Every time she closed her eyes she relived those searing kisses, so midnight found her wide awake, staring at the drifts of netting that festooned the bed.

Was Cade looking for an affair? Just thinking about that made her heart jump nervously and stirred her senses into humming awareness.

If so, she'd refuse him. He'd accept that—and, even if he didn't, she didn't need to worry about her safety, because he wasn't the sort of man to force her.

Repressing a shudder at old memories, she wondered why she was so sure.

For one thing, the blonde woman in her skimpy black shift would be only too eager to indulge him if all he wanted was a quick fling. And, judging by various covert glances Taryn had intercepted, several other women at dinner wouldn't mind being seduced by his muscled elegance and magnetic impact.

But what convinced her was his restraint, his complete self-discipline when he'd kissed her. She'd dissolved into a puddle of sensation, and he'd known it, but he'd not tried to persuade her into bed.

Her physical safety was not an issue.

So how about her emotions? Was she falling in love?

Restlessness forced her out from the tumbled sheets. She pushed back a swathe of filmy mosquito netting and walked across to the window, staring out at a tropical fantasy in silver and black, the moon's path across the lagoon as bright as the stars in the Milky Way.

No, this passionate madness had very little to do with love. Love needed time; it had taken her several months to realise she loved Antony.

She let the curtain drop and went back to bed. That love, however sincere, hadn't been enough, and she'd been sufficiently scarred to believe she lacked passion. She'd accepted Antony's disillusioned statements as truths.

Possibly that was why she hadn't seen anything more than cheerful camaraderie in Peter's attitude to her.

Bitterly, uselessly, she rued her mistaken impression that he'd been joking when he'd asked her to marry him. She was still haunted by her last sight of him—smiling as she'd waved goodbye and turned into the Departures area of the airport.

A few hours later he was dead. Why? The often-asked question hammered pitilessly at her.

Why hadn't he confided in her? They'd been friends—*good* friends—and she might have been able to help.

Oh, who was she kidding? Peter hadn't wanted friendship; he'd wanted love. If she'd given in to his pleading she'd have been replaying the wretchedness of her engagement, because she hadn't desired him—not as she desired Cade...

Cade's presence had pushed memories of Peter to the back of her mind. He was vital, compelling in a way that completely overshadowed Peter. Guilt lay like a heavy weight on her mind, in her heart—an emotion she'd never appease.

She sighed, turning to push the sheet back from her sticky body. The netting swayed in the flower-scented breeze. She felt heavy and hungry, aching with a need so potent she felt it in every cell.

Cade—tall and dark, and almost forbidding in his uncompromising masculinity, yet capable of consideration. Cade, who possibly wanted an affair.

Cade, who made her body sing like nothing she'd ever experienced before...

A stray thought drifted by, silken with forbidden temptation. What if she embarked on an affair with him?

She didn't dare risk it.

And why, when she'd loved Antony, had his passion never stirred her as Cade's kisses did? Dreamily, she recalled how it felt to be locked in Cade's arms, shivering with eager delight.

When sleep finally claimed her it was long after midnight. The next thing she knew was a voice saying incisively, 'Taryn, wake up!'

She opened her eyes, blinked at a steel-blue gaze and bolted upright. 'Wha—?'

'You've overslept,' Cade said curtly, and turned and left the room.

Stunned, still lost in the dream she'd been enjoying, Taryn stared around her.

Why hadn't her alarm gone off?

Leaning over, she pushed back the hair from her face so she could check, only to bite back a shocked word and twist off the bed.

She hadn't heard the alarm because last night she'd forgotten to set it.

And she'd forgotten to set it because she'd been too dazzled by Cade's kisses to think straight.

So much for professionalism!

Not only that, she'd kicked off her bedclothes. She was sprawled on top of the sheet in a pair of boxer shorts and a skimpy singlet top that had ridden sideways, revealing almost every inch of skin from her waist to her shoulders.

All of which Cade would have been able to see through the fine drift of mosquito netting.

Hot with delayed embarrassment, she dived across the room, performed her ablutions, changed into a businesslike shirt and skirt and walked out into the living room with her chin at an angle and every nerve taut.

Cade was standing at the table checking out a sheaf of papers.

'Sorry,' she said rapidly.

He lifted his head and gave her a long, cool look. Last night's kisses—and whether he'd just seen more of her than was *respectable*—clearly meant nothing to him.

All thought was blotted out by a stark, fierce surge of hunger when he crossed the room towards her. Desperately clinging to her splintering composure, she tried to ignore the powerful, masculine grace of his movements and the erratic beat of her heart.

'Jet lag reveals itself in different ways,' he said laconically. 'Here's what I want you to do after you've had breakfast.'

She forced herself to concentrate, only to be startled when he finished by saying, 'Drink plenty of water today and try a nap after lunch. It might help.' He looked at his watch. 'I have to go. I'll be back around midday.'

Taryn took a deep breath, letting it out on an explosive sigh once she was safely alone.

'Breakfast,' she said to the silent room, then started at a knock on the door. Fortunately, it heralded a delicious concoction of tropical fruit with good toast to back it up.

And excellent coffee... Mentally thanking that long-ago Arabian—or had he been Ethiopian?—goatherd who'd noticed how frisky his goats became after grazing on coffee berries, she ate breakfast before setting to work.

Although she still felt a little slack and listless, by the time the sun was at its highest she'd finished nearly everything Cade had set out for her.

When he arrived back in the *fale* he glanced at her work. 'Thank you. This is just what I need. I'm having a working lunch but you can eat here or in the restaurant, whichever you prefer.'

'Here,' she said.

Cade's nod was short, almost dismissive. 'And take that nap.'

Clearly he regretted those feverish kisses as much as she did.

Perhaps for him they hadn't been feverish. Had he been taken aback—even dismayed—by the intensity of her response?

Even if he hadn't, his aloofness was understandable; basically, he was indicating that although he'd forgotten himself enough to kiss her, he regretted it and she wasn't to presume on it.

Kiss in haste, repent at leisure—a classic case of the morning after the night before, she thought, smarting with something close to shame.

Ignoring the tight knot in her stomach, she worked through lunch, and afterwards followed instructions to take a short nap, only to wake with heavy limbs and a threatening headache.

A swim in the lagoon revived her considerably. On her way back to the *fale*, she met the Frenchwoman with impeccable style who'd admired her *pareu* the previous evening.

Beside her was a much younger woman, a stunning opera singer. After giving Taryn an indifferent nod, she began to complain of boredom.

Madame Murat listened to her complaints with a smile, before saying, 'It would be my dream to spend the rest of my life in this lovely place.' She looked at Taryn. 'You, my dear, are here to work, are you not?'

'Yes.' Taryn added brightly, 'But working in paradise is no effort.'

The younger woman gave a significant smile. 'No effort at all when you're sharing...' she paused, before adding on a husky laugh '...*accommodation* with a hunk like Cade Peredur. Lucky you.' Another pause, before she asked, 'What's he like—as an employer, I mean, of course.'

'Very professional,' Taryn said woodenly.

'How maddening for you,' the other woman said, odiously sympathetic. She gazed around the shimmering lagoon and pulled a petulant face. 'I didn't realise we were going to be stuck on this tiny little dot of land all the time we were here.'

After a nod to each of them, she walked away. The Frenchwoman said tolerantly, 'Poor girl— she had hopes of a resort holiday, I think, with handsome men to admire her and a chance to display her jewels. Instead, there are only other wives while our men are working.' She glanced past Taryn. 'Ah, here comes your employer. They must have finished talking for the afternoon.'

Startled, Taryn looked up. Sunlight shafted down between the palms in swords of gold, tiger-striping Cade's lean, powerful form as he strode towards them. Her heart fluttered and her body sang into forbidden warmth as the memory of his kisses sparked a rush of tantalising adrenalin. She blinked against suddenly intense colours, so bright that even behind her sunglasses they dazzled.

Unexpectedly, the woman beside her said, 'Wise of you not to move, my dear. Unless you love him and know it is returned, never run towards a man. This one is coming to you as fast as he can.'

Flushing, Taryn said swiftly, 'He's my employer, that's all.'

'So far, and you are wise not to surrender too soon.' Her companion smiled wryly. 'My children say I am very old-fashioned, but I do not approve of modern attitudes. There should be some mystery in a love affair, some greater excitement than finding out how good in bed a man—or woman—is. A meeting of minds as well as of bodies.' Just before Cade came within earshot, she finished,

'And this man—both mind and body—would be a very interesting one to explore.'

She bestowed a frankly appreciative glance on him as he came to a stop before them and in a voice coloured by amusement she said, 'I hope you do not intend to scold your charming secretary for spending time with an old woman.'

The smile he gave her held cynicism, but was warmed by male appreciation for her soignée chic and elegant femininity. 'I don't see any old women around,' he said, 'and the days of wage slavery are long gone. Taryn would soon put me in my place if I tried to keep her immured in work.'

Madame Murat chuckled and steered the conversation into a discussion of the Pacific economy but, when Taryn admitted ruefully to knowing very little about that, adding that she'd been in London for the past couple of years, the older woman changed the subject to her favourite sights there.

None of them, Taryn thought when she was walking back to their suite with Cade, were sophisticated 'in' places; the older woman had concentrated on museums, galleries and parks—the sort of spots a tourist would be likely to visit.

'Do you like Madame Murat?' Cade surprised her by asking.

'Yes.' It came out too abruptly. She was too aware of him, of his intimidating assurance—and gripped by memories of the compelling sensuality of his kisses.

After clearing her throat, she said, 'Very much.'

His smile was narrow. 'She was fishing.'

Startled, she glanced at him. 'You mean—'

She stopped when she met his cool, cynical gaze. Yes, he did mean it. It hurt to think that the charming Frenchwoman might have targeted her.

He shrugged. 'She was laying ground bait. Her husband is very enthusiastic about a scheme I'm positive will fail, and he's almost certainly suggested she find out what you know of my plans.'

'I don't know anything of your plans,' she said shortly, angry with him for some obscure reason.

'And, even if I did, I do know how to hold my tongue.'

'I'm sure you do,' he returned smoothly, 'but it's always best to be forewarned. What's the matter?'

'Nothing.' When he sent her an ironically disbelieving glance, she enlarged reluctantly, 'Just that I liked her. It sounds ridiculous and overdramatic, but…it feels like a betrayal.'

Cade's eyes were keen. 'Of course you like her—she's a charming woman and a very intelligent one. She and her husband make a formidable team. She won't hold your discretion against you, and might well be useful to you in the future. As for betrayal—' His shoulders lifted and fell. 'It happens.'

Thoughtfully, Taryn said, 'I don't think I like your world much.'

A black brow lifted. 'My world, your world—what's the difference? Every world has its share of innocents and those who prey on them, of honest people and scoundrels. Unless you understand that, you run risks wherever you are.'

Shocked, she asked directly, 'Don't you trust anyone?'

Cade didn't answer straightaway. When the silence stretched too long, she looked up into an austere, unyielding mask.

He gave another barely noticeable shrug. 'A few. And only when they've proved trustworthy. Do you trust everyone you meet?'

After a moment's pause, she said, 'Of course not. Only a fool would do that.'

'And you're not a fool.'

A note in his voice made her uneasy. 'I try not to be,' she returned, irritated by her defensive tone.

The conversation was too personal—almost as personal as his kisses—and, strangely, she felt he was attacking her, trying to find some hidden weak spot he could use.

Don't be silly, she scoffed. *He's just making sure you can be trusted not to give away secrets...*

He asked, 'Did you manage to get some sleep after lunch?'

Hugely relieved at the change of subject, she said, 'Yes, for a short time.'

'I found your notes. You did a good job.'

She tried to suppress a warm pleasure. 'Thank you. I assume there's more.'

'Yes, although I don't need it until tomorrow afternoon. Have you ever been to the main island?'

'Only yesterday when we arrived,' she said dryly.

'In a couple of days I plan to check out the local fishing industry and I'd like you to come with me.'

Taryn said, 'All right. Do you want me to take notes? I can't do shorthand, but I could take notes by hand, or talk into a recorder—or even use the laptop.'

'I've got a recording device you can use. And I won't force you to trek around fishing factories or dirty, smelly boats,' he told her. 'We'll be meeting with the people who run the show, not the fishermen.'

She gave him a swift, amused look. 'I bet I've been in more dirty, smelly boats than you have.'

Cade liked her frankness—a little too much,

he conceded sardonically. It could have been an indication of inner honesty—except that she'd shown a chilling lack of empathy for Peter.

Could that have been because of her crass fiancé? He must have been a total fool, because she certainly wasn't frigid by nature.

Quelling a sharp shock of desire, Cade banished the memory of her incandescent response to his kisses. It could have been faked, of course. Unpleasantly aware of a desire to find excuses for her behaviour to Peter, he had to remember to keep an open mind.

'You've spent a lot of time on such vessels?' he enquired as they approached the gardens that shielded their *fale* from the others on the island.

She grinned. 'My parents and I used to spend the holidays travelling for a charity that sent medical aid to the islands. We sailed mostly on traders—and trust me, although they did their best, those vessels smelt and they were quite often dirty. The tropics can make things difficult for anyone with a cleanliness fetish.'

'You didn't think of following your parents into medicine?' he asked casually.

'Yes, but it didn't work out.'

'Why?'

She shrugged, her breasts beneath the *pareu* moving freely. Cade's groin tightened. Seeing her almost naked in her bed that morning meant he knew exactly what the brightly coloured fabric covered. He had to dismiss an image of his hands removing the thin cotton that covered her, then lingering across the satin-skinned curves he'd revealed.

Without looking at him, Taryn said, 'About halfway through my first year of pre-med study I realised that I simply didn't have the desire or the passion. It was my parents' dream for me, not mine.'

'How did they feel about that?'

Her narrow brows met for a second. 'They weren't happy,' she admitted, her tone cool and matter-of-fact. 'I felt really bad about it, but I couldn't see myself being a good doctor. For me, medicine would have been just a job.'

'Whereas for them it's a vocation?'

Her surprised glance sparked irritation in Cade, an emotion that fought with the swift leap of his blood when she turned her head away and the sun transformed her wet red locks into a coppery-gold aureole.

Clearly she hadn't thought him capable of recognising altruism. For some reason he wasn't prepared to examine, that stung.

'Yes,' she said simply. 'They made big sacrifices for me. Because they wanted to give me a good secondary education, they came back to New Zealand and bought the practice at Aramuhu. As soon as they'd organised me into university, they went back to the islands.'

Cade felt an odd, almost unwilling sympathy. Although philanthropic, her parents seemed to have been as casual about her as his mother had been. Had traipsing around after them on their missions of mercy given her a distaste for a lifetime of service?

It bothered him that he didn't blame her.

Her chin lifted and her green-gold eyes met his with a direct challenge. She said firmly, 'So I studied for librarian qualifications—much more my thing.'

'And you've not regretted it?'

'Not a bit.' In the dark shelter of one of the big raintrees, Taryn sneaked an upward glance. Nothing showed in his expression but casual interest, yet her voice tightened so she had to hurry over her final remark. 'My parents are perfectly happy with the way I've organised my life, and so am I.'

In any other man, she'd have accepted his words as idle chit-chat, the small coin of communication, but she was pretty certain Cade didn't do casual. When he asked a question, he really wanted the answer.

A hot little thrill shivered through her as they walked out into the sun again. His kisses had indicated one sort of awareness, but did this conversation mean he felt more for her than uncomplicated lust?

Startled by a swift, passionate yearning that went deeper than desire, far deeper than anything she'd experienced before, she blinked and pretended to examine the shrubs beside the path.

Those hard eyes saw too much and, although she didn't understand him in any real way, somehow he stirred a secret, unsuspected part of her. She longed to warm herself in the intense primal heat she sensed behind the uncompromising exterior he presented to the world.

Abruptly, she stopped walking. Keeping her face turned away from Cade, she touched a hibiscus flower, letting her fingertips linger on the brilliant satin petals. It took all her self-possession to say in a level voice, 'Only a flower could get away with this combination—vivid orange petals with a heart as bright and dark as a ruby. The colours should clash hideously, but somehow they don't.'

Control restored, she lifted her hand and turned back to him, insides curling when she realised he wasn't looking at the bloom. Instead, his gaze was fixed on her mouth. Sensation ricocheted through her, tantalising and tempting.

Without haste, he said, 'It's all part of the forbidden, fated lure of the tropics, I believe.'

'Forbidden? Fated?' She let the flower go and resumed walking. In her most prosaic tone, she said, 'The European sailors who first explored these islands thought they'd found paradise.'

'Ask Luke Chapman to tell you about the first Chapman who arrived in Fala'isi. His story might change your mind about that.'

'Oh, the Polynesians were warlike, of course,' she admitted, keeping her voice practical. 'But they were hugely hospitable too, and although there were episodes when the two cultures clashed badly—like Captain Cook's death in Hawaii— they weren't common.'

Wanting Cade Peredur was asking for trouble. Better to keep her distance, stay safe behind the barricades, not waste her time and emotional energy on a man who—at the most—would suggest an affair.

Probably one as brief as tropical twilight, and with as little impact on him.

And there was always the possibility that her body was playing tricks on her, luring her on with a promise it couldn't fulfil. In spite of Cade's kisses, if they made love her desire might evaporate as swiftly as it had with Antony. She could do without a repeat of that humiliation.

Mouth firming, she bade her erratic heartbeat to settle down as they reached the *fale*.

'Those first explorers called them the Isles of Aphrodite,' he said, surprising her again. 'Love has to be the most dangerous emotion in the world.'

Her brows shot up. 'Dangerous? I can see that sometimes it might be,' she conceded. 'But fated and forbidden? That's a bit extreme. Plenty of people fall in love and live more or less happily ever after.'

'Plenty don't. And love has caused huge amounts of angst and misery.'

'Like any extreme emotion,' she agreed, heart twisting as she thought of Peter. Trying to ignore the sad memories and guilt, she said quietly, 'But there are different kinds of love. The love of parents for their children, for instance. Without that, the world would be a terrible place.'

Cade's face froze. 'Indeed,' he said evenly.

What had she said that had hit a nerve?

CHAPTER EIGHT

FOR a highly uncomfortable few seconds Cade looked at Taryn from narrowed eyes before asking abruptly, 'So what do you plan to do once you're back in New Zealand?'

'Find a proper job.' She grabbed at her composure and, once they were in the cool sitting room of the *fale*, said daringly, 'I'm thinking of asking you for a reference about my research abilities.'

'I expected as much.' His voice was level and lacking in emotion. And then he drawled, 'However, I'll need a little more experience of your skills before I can give you a reference that would mean anything.'

The words were innocuous enough—quite reasonable, in fact—but a note in his voice set her teeth on edge.

Meeting eyes that were narrowed and intent, she said crisply, 'I don't like the sound of that.'

His brows lifted. 'Why?'

Wishing too late she hadn't opened her mouth, Taryn knew she had to go on. 'Because that almost sounded like the sort of thing a sleazy employer might say to a defenceless employee.'

The half beat of silence tightened her nerves to screaming point, until he laughed with what seemed like genuine amusement.

'You're far from defenceless,' he said coolly, 'and I rather resent you suggesting I'm sleazy. If you need the reassurance, any reference I write for you will be based entirely on your work, which so far I've found to be excellent.'

'Thank you,' she contented herself with saying.

He asked in that objective voice she was beginning to distrust, 'You're a beautiful woman. Do you have to set boundaries whenever you take a new position?'

'No.' Too brusque, but she wasn't going to elaborate.

However, he said, 'But you have had to before.'

'Do I act as though I expect every employer to try to jump me?'

His look of distaste made her stiffen and brace herself.

He said, 'No, but it's clear that you've developed ways to defend yourself. Unsurprising, really, since your parents deserted you once you left school.'

His tone hadn't altered, which somehow made his statement even more startling. Taryn said indignantly, 'I wasn't deserted! We kept in touch all the time—if I'd needed them, they'd have been there for me. They still are.'

One black brow lifted, something she realised happened whenever he didn't believe her. 'How long is it since you've seen them?'

She paused before admitting, 'A couple of years.'

'It sounds pretty close to being abandoned.'

'No, you don't understand—'

'I understand abandonment.' His voice was coldly deliberate. 'My birth father I never knew. My mother abandoned me at birth to be brought up by my grandmother. When she died, I lived with my mother, but I was eventually taken into care. I lived—happily—with foster parents after that, but recently I've lost my foster-brother.'

Shocked and horrified at what her innocent words had summoned, Taryn said quietly, 'Yes, you obviously do understand abandonment, and I'm very sorry for that, but my parents haven't abandoned me. I'm a big girl now, Cade—Mr Peredur—and quite capable of looking after myself without needing them to shepherd me through life.'

'Oh, call me Cade,' he said negligently. 'We might not have been introduced formally but last night in my arms you called me Cade without hesitation.'

Colour burning through her skin, she said, 'I haven't thanked you for making sure that fruit bat didn't blunder into me.'

He shrugged. 'At the time I thought it was a fallen coconut I was rescuing you from. You've been digging trenches and laying barbed wire along your defences since you woke up this morning. Why? Because we kissed?'

'Of course not.' Immediately she'd spoken, she

wondered if she should have told him the exact opposite.

Then he wouldn't have smiled—the cool, easy smile of a conqueror—and lifted his hand. Her eyes widened endlessly in fascinated apprehension, but all he did was push back a lock of sea-damp hair that clung to her cheek. His fingers barely grazed her skin, yet she felt their impact like a caress, silkily sliding through her body to melt every inhibition.

Dropping his hand, he said, 'It's quite simple, Taryn. If you don't want me to touch you, all you need to do is say so.'

Neither his face nor his tone revealed any emotion beyond a wry amusement.

She resisted the need to lick suddenly dry lips. Cade's touch had paralysed her, banishing everything but a swift, aching pleasure from his nearness. He filled her gaze, blotting out the seductive lure of the tropical afternoon with a potent male magnetism that sapped both her energy and her will.

Again Cade held out his hand but this time, instead of touching her, he waited, his expression

cool and challenging. Desire—hot and irresistible—pulsed through her, overwhelming her fears
in a honeyed flow she felt in every cell in her
body. He was watching her with an intensity that
was more seductive than any caress or polished
words, as though she were the most important
thing in his life.

Slowly, eyes locked with the steel-sheen-blue
of his, she fought a losing battle against the impulse to take what he was offering and ignore the
common sense that urged her to say no.

Yet she didn't say it. Couldn't say it.

'What is this?' The words stumbled huskily
from her, almost meaningless, yet he seemed to
know what she wanted from him.

He said, 'You must know—since last night,
if not before—that I find you very attractive.
And you seem to reciprocate. But, if you're not
interested, all you have to do is refuse. However,
if I'm right and this—' his mouth twisted
'—*attraction* is mutual, then we should decide
what to do about it.'

Plain words. Too plain. And he knew damned
well that the attraction was mutual! For a moment

she suffered a pang of angry rebellion. Why didn't he woo her with passion, with heady kisses?

She knew the reason. Because he wanted her to know that whatever he felt was not love, not even a romance. He'd made it quite clear—he trusted no one. If she succumbed, it would be a business affair with no promises made and no hearts broken, just a clean cut when it was over.

Her only sensible response must be that simple syllable of refusal.

Yet still it wouldn't come.

Would succumbing to his offer be so dangerous...?

Or would it finally free her from fear, from the poisonous aftermath of Antony's violence?

Fighting a honeyed, treacherous temptation, Taryn searched for something sensible to say, words to get her out of the situation before she got too tangled in her rioting emotions.

None came.

She glanced upwards. As usual, she couldn't read anything in the arrogant features. Indignantly, she thought that his enigmatic look would be etched into her memory for ever.

In the end, she said as steadily as she could, 'In other words, why don't we both scratch an itch?'

Cade inspected her from the top of her head to her toes, his cryptic gaze fanning that treacherous desire deep inside her.

But when he spoke his voice held nothing but detachment. 'If that's how you see it, then yes.'

She bristled, made angry by a foolish, obscure pain.

Still in that judicial tone, he continued, 'But for me there's more to it than that. I've met a lot of beautiful women. I don't believe many—if any—would have held that hose and, in spite of knowing she hadn't a hope of doing it, still tried to stop the forest going up in flames.'

And, while she silently digested that, he went on, 'I want you. Not just because you make my pulse leap whenever you come into the room, but because I find you intriguing and I enjoy your company.' His broad shoulders sketched a shrug. 'If you want a declaration of undying love I can't give it to you. I know it exists—I just don't seem to be able to feel it myself. Why are you shaking your head?'

'I'm not asking for that.' Yet she hated the thought of being just another in the parade of women through his life.

He frowned. 'Then what do you want?'

'I don't know.' She hesitated, before adding in a troubled voice, 'To be reassured, I suppose—and I don't even know what I mean by that, but it makes me sound horribly needy and clinging, which I am not.'

'You most emphatically are not,' he agreed dryly. 'Well, what is it to be?'

When she didn't answer, he said in an entirely different voice, 'I could kiss you into agreement.'

Taryn opened her mouth to deny it, then closed her lips over the lying words.

Quietly, he said, 'So which will it be?'

Her thoughts tumbled in delirious free fall. Making love to Cade would be a step into a wildly stimulating unknown. Yet, in spite of being convinced she'd respond to Cade's lovemaking as eagerly as she had to his kisses, at the back of her mind lurked the dark cloud of apprehension that had been her constant companion since her engagement.

Now was a chance—perhaps her only chance—to find out whether she could be what Antony had called *a real woman*—one who enjoyed passion and could give herself in that most fundamental way.

And what harm could possibly come from a short affair when both she and Cade knew the rules?

None at all, that reckless inner part of her urged. Love had no part in this, so she'd be unscathed when the time came for them to part. And if—*if* she could surrender to desire fully and without shame, she'd be free at last of humiliation and able to consider an equal relationship some time in the future.

Slowly, reluctantly, she lifted her eyes and met Cade's gaze, which was narrowed with desire—for *her*—and, as she thrilled with a potent, spontaneous surge of sensuous hunger, she knew her answer.

If she didn't take this opportunity, she'd always

regret her cowardice. Whatever happened, even if it ended in tears and heartache, she was desperately in thrall to a need she didn't want to resist.

But her voice wobbled when she said, 'I... Then it's yes.'

Cade fought back a fierce satisfaction—so fierce it startled him. With it came a driving, insistent hunger and something he'd never expected to feel—an intense need he immediately tried to block.

Because it was still too soon. Those enormous green-gold eyes and her soft trembling mouth certainly betrayed desire, but he sensed fear too.

For the first time in his life a headstrong passion had almost overridden his mind and his will. If he took her now he could wreck everything. She needed to be sure of his ability to rouse her, confidence that he wouldn't hurt her before she could come to him without restrictions, without fear or shame.

She needed gentling. Wooing...

He needed to know her better.

He shied away from that thought. And he, he

thought grimly, needed to find a way to control this almost desperate sexual drive.

Watching her so he could gauge her reaction, he said with as much resolution as he could muster, 'It's all right, I'm not going to drag you off into a bedroom right now.'

'I didn't think you would,' she returned smartly. 'I'm sure your motto is always business first.'

He permitted himself a narrow, humourless smile—probably looking more like a tiger ready to pounce, he thought with grim humour. 'So why are you still holding yourself as stiffly as a martyr facing the stake?'

'I'm not!' But she was; already she could feel her shoulders start to ache.

And Cade's response didn't relax her at all. 'You need time to get to know me better,' he said.

Taryn paused, her mind racing against the thud of her heartbeats. In the end she nodded. 'Yes, I do,' she admitted, chagrin colouring her voice. 'Everything's happened so fast I feel as though I've been whisked off by a tornado. And you obviously need time too.'

'I know what I want.' He gave another of those

twisted smiles, as though he understood the riot of emotions clouding her thoughts. 'It's all right, Taryn. There will come a time when we both know it's right. Until then, we'll carry on as we have been.'

Abruptly, that shaming relief fled, to be replaced by a disappointment so acute she almost changed her mind there and then. But he was right, she thought, clinging to a shred of common sense. She needed time.

He glanced at his watch, then out into the western sky, already lit with the pageantry of a tropical sunset. 'If we're going to be in time for the dinner cruise on the lagoon we'd better get going.'

Business first, of course, she thought as she nodded and hurried into her room, frustrated yet relieved. Her insides quivered. If only she didn't freeze…

Then she thought of what she'd learned about him, and her heart shuddered. She wanted to know so much more than the few spare statements he'd delivered in that chillingly impersonal tone, but the thought of him as a child, at the mercy of a neglectful mother, hurt her in an almost physical way.

No time for that now, she told herself after a harried glance at her watch. What to wear? The gold *pareu* again? Not entirely suitable for sailing—although the vessel that had anchored in the lagoon that morning looked more like a miniliner than a yacht.

A swift search through her wardrobe made her decide on a gift from her mother. Pacific in style, the loose top of fine, silky cotton echoed the colours of handmade *tapa* cloth. Its soft cream-white fabric, patterned in chocolate-brown, tan and bronze, made her skin glow. With it, she wore sleek tan trousers and a cuff bracelet of tiny golden mother-of-pearl beads.

When she reappeared Cade gave her a swift smouldering look. Her stomach swooped and colour surged along her cheekbones. She had to steady her voice before she could say, 'I hope this is OK.'

He said, 'Infinitely more than merely OK. You look radiant. We'd better get going or I'll succumb to temptation and try to persuade you to skip the damned evening.'

A stripped, corrosive note in his words lit fires deep inside her.

Some hours later, Taryn leaned against the rail of the opulent vessel, which was owned by one of the most powerful businessmen in Australia.

She'd had an interesting evening. She'd been admired, patronised and ignored; she'd been entertained by Madame Murat, who'd revealed a charmingly indiscreet side that made Taryn chuckle; she'd fended off attempts at flirtation by various men and she'd eaten a delicious Pacific buffet meal beside Cade. He'd shown no overt possessiveness, but he'd clearly been keeping an eye on her.

She turned as someone came towards her, stabbed by sharp, unexpected disappointment when she saw not Cade but the son of the yacht owner. Tall and cheerfully laconic, he'd made no secret of his interest.

'Alone?' he said against the babble of talk and laughter from the big entertaining deck. 'Are we boring you?'

'No. I'm admiring the skies.'

He stopped just a little too close beside her. 'They're stunning, but if you want fabulous you should come to the Outback. Nothing beats the stars over the Australian desert. Check them out one day—we've got a cattle station so remote you'd think there was nowhere else on earth. I'd like to take you star-watching there.'

'It sounds amazing,' she told him, keeping her voice non-committal. A flurry of white in the water caught her attention. 'Oh—what was that?'

'What?'

When he turned to see where she was pointing out she took the opportunity to move along the rail away from him. 'A splash—perhaps dolphins jumping? I presume there must be dolphins here.'

'Might be a whale,' he said, examining the water. He gestured towards a waiter, who came rapidly towards them. 'Binoculars, please,' he said, and turned back to her. 'Sounds as though you're used to dolphins jumping around you when you swim.'

'Not exactly,' she said, 'although pods often turn up off the coast of my part of Northland.'

He smiled down at her. 'What part of Northland? The Bay of Islands?'

'A bit farther north than that,' she said vaguely. He was good-looking and charming in an open, friendly way. Normally, she'd have flirted happily enough with him. But this wasn't normality; nothing had been normal since last night when Cade had kissed her and tilted her world off its axis.

The arrival of the waiter with binoculars eased things. 'Try these,' her companion said, offering them to her.

She squinted into them and suddenly caught a pod of dolphins arching up from the water in a free-wheeling display of gymnastics, graceful and joyous and gleaming in the starshine.

'Oh, lovely,' she breathed, turning to hand over the binoculars, only to discover her companion was now standing behind her, so close she actually turned into him.

'I'll get out of your way,' she said crisply and

thrust the binoculars into his hands, ducking sideways.

Cade came striding towards them. Something about him made her stiffen; behind him, a group of people watched, clearly intrigued. Without thinking, she lifted her hand and beckoned, then pointed out to sea where the dolphins played.

'Dolphins,' she said, hoping her smile conveyed nothing more than simple pleasure.

The man beside her took the binoculars away from his eyes. 'They look as though they're moving away.' He looked beyond her, his demeanour subtly altering when he saw Cade approach.

'Hi, mate, take a look at this,' he said, handing him the binoculars. 'We'll go across to them so everyone can see them close up.'

'No, don't do that,' Taryn said swiftly.

Both men looked at her. 'Why?' Cade asked.

'At home we're told not to interfere with them—it disturbs them, especially if they have young with them. If they come across to us of their own accord, that's fine, but deliberately seeking them out isn't.'

Both men looked at each other, then the Australian grinned. 'OK, anything for a pretty lady. I'll get them to break out all the binoculars on board.'

Cade waited until he'd gone before checking out the dolphins.

Eyes narrowing as she watched the sea creatures, Taryn said, 'They look as though they've turned—they are heading this way, aren't they?'

'It seems so.' He lowered the binoculars and looked at her. 'Enjoying yourself?'

'Yes, thank you. It's a fantastic night and the food is delicious, and the people are very pleasant.'

As well as Fleur and Luke Chapman, she'd recognised a couple of business tycoons from New Zealand, one with his wife, a Mediterranean princess. A media baron and his fourth wife were in a huddle with several politicians from countries around the Pacific Rim, and an exquisite rill of laughter came from the opera star as she flirted with her husband.

Which made a change from flirting with Cade,

Taryn thought waspishly. She said, 'Everywhere I look, I see faces from the television screen.'

And they all seemed to know each other well; she was the only outsider.

Just then someone else saw the dolphins, now close to the yacht, and called out, and there was a concerted move to the rails.

Taryn said, 'We'll get the best view up in the bows.'

Cade examined her face for a brief second, then nodded. 'Let's go.'

Several people followed them. Taryn tried hard not to wish she could stand alone with Cade in the moonlight watching the glorious creatures ride the bow wave with consummate grace, their curving mouths giving them the appearance of high delight. Silver veils of water garlanded their rounded, muscular backs while they dipped and pirouetted and leapt from the water, gleeful and wild in their unforced joy.

And then, as quickly as they'd come, an un- heard command sent them speeding away to an unknown destination. And people who'd been lost in silent wonder broke out into a babble of noise that broke the spell.

Cade said, 'What was that sigh for?'

'Anything beautiful makes me feel sad—in an odd, delighted way,' she said, then laughed. 'They're such magnificent creatures, so wild and free, and they seem to get a huge kick out of wave-riding. You could just *feel* their pleasure, couldn't you?'

He nodded, his eyes searching as he looked down at her. 'I'm glad you saw them.'

Taryn would have enjoyed the rest of the evening much more if anticipation hadn't been tightening inside her, straining her nerves and clamouring for the evening to end so that she could go back to the *fale* with Cade.

However, once they were alone, he closed the door and turned to her, eyes narrowed and gleaming, his face a mask of intent. She felt a sudden clutch of panic.

'You seemed to have a good time,' he said.

She nodded. 'Did you?'

'No.' His smile was brief and mirthless. 'I kept having to stop myself from striding over and establishing territorial rights every time I saw some man head in your direction.'

Taryn's hiccup of laughter was cut short when he slipped his tie free and dropped it, then shrugged out of his jacket. 'Surely you couldn't have thought that—'

She stopped, watching the way the powerful muscles flexed and coiled beneath his white shirt. Her breath came short between her lips. In a voice she didn't recognise she admitted, 'I understand the feeling.'

He looked at her and said in a completely different tone, 'All night I've been wondering whether that elegant and very suitable garment is as easy to remove as it seems to be. One night I'll find out. And if you want me to keep to our agreement, you'd better get into your room right now.'

Taryn dragged her gaze from his, blinked several times and said in a muted voice, 'Goodnight.'

She heard him laugh as she closed the bedroom door behind her, the low laugh of a man who had his life in order.

The three days that followed were a lesson in sorely tried patience and silent escalating tension.

In public Cade treated her with an understated awareness. In private he touched her—her hand, her shoulder, an arm slipped around her waist occasionally.

Taryn knew what he was doing—getting her accustomed to his touch, his nearness, like a nervous filly being broken to the saddle. And the subtle courtship worked; each touch eased her fears, set up a yearning that grew with the hours until she found herself dreaming of him, an erotic dream that woke her into a shivering hunger unlike anything she'd ever known.

Twisting onto her side, she stared past the misty swag of the netting into the warm night, and knew that for her the time of waiting was over.

Her breath eased, but restlessness drove her to switch on the bedside lamp and pick up her watch. Almost midnight—not called the witching hour for nothing, she thought and switched off the light, settling back against the pillows.

Only to toss sleeplessly. Eventually, she got out of bed and opened the screens onto the terrace.

The air outside was marginally cooler against her skin.

A blur of movement froze her into stillness.

CHAPTER NINE

IT WAS Cade, gazing out at the night. He turned to watch her as she stood in the doorway. A silver bar of moonlight revealed the strong male contours of his face and the fact that he was still fully clothed.

He didn't speak. Very much aware of her skimpy singlet top and shorts, Taryn swallowed to ease a suddenly dry throat and said abruptly, 'I've had enough time.'

Almost expressionless, a muscle in his jaw twitched as he held out his hand. 'So come to me.'

Taryn looked at him, toughly formidable, his handsome face almost unyielding in its bold angularity. He radiated power and an uncompromising male authority that should have warned her not to push.

Instead, it evoked something close to defiance.

He was so clearly accustomed to being in charge, to taking women on his terms, not theirs.

'You come to me,' she returned and, although each word was soft and slightly hesitant, there could be no mistaking the challenge in both words and tone, in her level gaze and the tilt of her chin.

She expected some resistance and was startled when his beautiful mouth curled into an appreciative smile. Noiselessly, he walked across the terrace and, without any further comment, drew her to him, enfolding her as though she was precious to him.

Held against his lean, muscled length, she sighed and relaxed. It was too much like coming home. Lashes fluttering down, she hid her face in his shoulder, every sense languorously accepting and eager.

A finger under her chin lifted her face, gentle but inexorable.

'Look at me,' Cade said, his voice rough and deep.

But she couldn't—didn't dare. Panicking, she thought, *Don't be such an idiot. If looking at him seems too intimate, how are you going to make love with him?*

Shivers raced across her skin when she felt the warmth of his breath on her eyelids, and then the soft brush of his mouth across hers.

His voice was deep and low, pitched so only a lover would hear. 'Open your eyes, Taryn.'

When he repeated the command she slowly lifted her lashes to meet a hooded, glittering gaze that melted her spine.

Instantly, his arms locked around her, crushing her breasts against his broad chest, and the intimate contact of his thighs made her vividly, desperately aware of his arousal.

And her own. Need consumed her, tearing at her with insistent velvet claws. When his mouth came down on hers, she opened her lips to his bold claim and gave him what they both wanted— her surrender, joyous and open and exultant.

Eventually, when she was clinging and helpless with longing, he raised his head. Eyes glittering, he asked, 'Was that so difficult?'

'No,' she said on an outgoing breath and, before she could change her mind, 'But three days ago I should have told you I don't believe in one-night stands.'

Releasing her, he said calmly, 'Neither do I.'

He trusted very few people and presumably that applied to her too, but there was genuine understanding in his tone. He'd recognised the fears that swayed her—fears and caution that now seemed flimsy and foolish—and didn't think any the less of her for them.

Yet when he took her hand, she hesitated.

'Second thoughts, Taryn?' His voice was aloof.

She reached up and touched his jaw, fingertips thrilling at the slight tactile roughness there. Cade held her hand against his mouth and kissed the fingers that had stroked his skin.

'No,' she whispered. 'No second thoughts. I just need to know you'll respect me in the morning.' A tremulous smile belied the steadiness of her gaze.

Cade's eyes hardened. Tension thrummed between them, fierce and significant.

Until he bent his head and kissed the corner

of her mouth. 'Not a whit less than I respect you now,' he said deliberately.

Renewed confidence surged through her. She let him turn her and went with him into her room. Excitement beat through her, quickening as she turned to face him.

'Do you want the light on?' he asked, barely moving his lips.

'No.' She didn't want any other light than that of the moon, a silvery, shadowy glow full of mystery and magic.

Cade's eyes kindled into diamond-bright intensity, burning blue as the heart of a flame. 'You take my breath away,' he said gutturally and pulled off his shirt, dropping it onto the floor.

Taryn's breath stopped in her throat. He was utterly overwhelming, all fluid muscle and bronzed skin and heady male charisma. Acting on instinct, she reached out a tentative hand and skimmed his broad chest, fingertips tingling at the contrast of supple skin and the silken overlay of hair. Her heart pumped loudly in her ears and she sucked in a sharp breath at the raw, leashed strength that emanated from him, balanced by masculine grace and an aura of power.

She muttered, 'And you are…magnificent,' and pulled her little singlet top over her head.

Cade's mouth hardened. For a second she froze, her eyes fixed on his face, but when he kissed her, deeply and sensuously, taking his fill of her, she forgot everything but his mouth on hers and the hands that slid across her back to hold her upright when her knees would no longer carry her weight.

When the kiss was over he scrutinised her face, his glinting eyes narrowing in the taut silence while his hands moved again, one down to her hips, the other lingering to trace the curves of her breasts before finally, just when she thought the tension inside her would have to be released in a groan, he cupped them.

Stunned and charmed, she shivered as he bent his head and kissed an expectant tip.

Desire uncoiled through her so swiftly it shocked her. Nothing, she thought helplessly when he eased her across his arm so that he could take the pink crest of a breast into his mouth—*nothing* in her previous life had prepared her for this charged, voluptuous delight.

At the sensuous tug of his lips, erotic little shudders tightened her skin and she closed her eyes, swamped by the sheer immensity of the sensations sweeping through her.

Dimly, she realised that all her fears had been wasted—whatever had kept her from enjoying sex previously no longer applied. Shivering with a passionate intensity, she was transformed, taken over by a desperate craving for something she didn't recognise, didn't understand. Her back arched in unconscious demand, and Cade lifted his head and subjected her to a darkly probing survey.

Shaken by the hunger surging through her veins, she gasped as he eased her onto the bed. Colour burned through her skin and her lashes fluttered down when he stripped completely.

But once he came down beside her, she turned into him, seeking his strength to appease the hunger burning inside her. His arms tightened around her and he kissed the wildly beating pulse in her throat.

'Open your eyes.' It was a command, not a request.

She tried to steady her voice, force it into something like its normal sensible tone, but the words came out in a husky, languorous whisper. 'It's too much...'

'What is?' And when she didn't answer he bent his head again and his lips closed over the other tightly budding peak.

'Everything,' she croaked, her pulse racing so fast she thought she might faint with the delicious thrill of his caress.

By the time he'd eased her remaining garment from her she no longer remembered that once she'd lain frozen and repelled by just such a caress. His hand moved between her legs and he began to press rhythmically and without haste, setting up a powerful sensuous counterpoint to the exquisite tug of his mouth. Insistent, demanding pleasure built in the pit of her stomach, a driving, powerful ache totally beyond her experience.

'Look at me,' Cade breathed, lifting his head so that Taryn felt his lips brush against her breast with each word.

Molten rills of sensation raced through her—beautiful, devouring, possibly destructive fire, but it was too late to call a halt now.

Not that she would, even if she could. Heat from his body fanned her passionate reaction to the subtle masculine scent that was his alone, and the intoxicating seduction of his skilled caresses had gone straight to her head.

'I think I'm shy,' she muttered, not surprised when he laughed deep in his throat.

Except that a shy woman wouldn't have yielded so quickly, so easily.

She'd wanted Cade from the moment their eyes met, her body surrendering to an elemental hunger her mind had refused to recognise. That hidden, barely registered excitement had tangled logic and caution into knots, sneakily undermining them and persuading her she'd be perfectly safe going to Fala'isi with him.

'Shy?' he murmured, his voice thick. 'A little, perhaps, and tantalisingly elusive, but so intriguingly responsive.'

His fingers slid deeper, towards her acutely sensitive core, and suddenly desire fractured into light that filled every cell in her body with shimmering transcendent sensation, a rapture that took her totally by surprise.

Her lashes flew up. Hugely dilated shocked eyes locking with his, she came apart in his arms, so abandoned to the magic of Cade's lovemaking she had no defence against her wild surrender.

He silenced the gasp that escaped her with a kiss so fierce and sensual she didn't register the flare of satisfaction in his eyes. Her lashes drifted down and she lay cradled against him for several minutes while her heartbeat slowed into normality and the vivid consummation faded into the sweet laziness of sated desire.

Until Cade moved, positioning himself over her. Then, in a reaction she couldn't stop, her body tensed. Bleak despair roiled through her. Willing her muscles to relax, she had to force herself to meet the keen, polished steel of his gaze.

'It's all right,' he said abruptly. 'I won't hurt you.'

'I know.' Hardly breathing, she tried to unlock her muscles.

He bent and took her breast into his mouth

again. And somehow, miraculously, passion conquered fear, floating through her in pleasurable ripples that almost immediately coalesced into a mill race of urgent, clamorous anticipation.

Cade lifted his head, narrowly examining her face, then said, 'Yes?'

'Oh, yes,' she breathed.

Blue eyes held her gaze as he eased into her by slow, sensuous increments and began to move almost sinuously, his male strength and power controlled by a will she dimly recognised.

Hunger poured through her in a violent rush, easing his passage with a flood that summoned voluptuous tremors through her. Instantly gauging her response, he thrust more fiercely and she gasped again, hips arching off the bed to meet him, the carnal rhythm projecting her into a world where all she had to cling to was this heady, dazzling sensation and the driving measure of their hearts against each other.

Lost in rapture, almost immediately she crested again in an infinitely more complex, intense culmination that hurtled her through some unmarked boundary on a soaring wave of ecstasy. Just when she was certain she couldn't bear any more pleasure, his breathing became harsh and he flung back his head. Through barely open eyes she saw him reach his fulfilment, his arrogant face a drawn mask of sexual pleasure, every muscle in his body cording in hard tension.

Eventually, while the erotic satiation faded into a dreamy daze, Taryn tried to sort her scattered thoughts. Stupidly, strangely, she longed for some tenderness from him, some acceptance of their mutual ecstasy, but without speaking, he twisted away and settled beside her on his back.

Close, so close, yet not touching. And she needed his touch now, so much she felt the need aching through her.

'All right?' he asked, his voice rough.

Hold me, she almost begged, but a remnant of common sense barred the abject plea. Terrified she might betray herself by letting the words free, she whispered, 'I didn't know it could be like that.'

His mouth crooked in a humourless smile and, without speaking, he turned onto his side and scooped her against him. His chest lifted as he said, 'He must have been a crass fool, that fiancé of yours.'

'Oh, no,' she said quietly. 'He loved me. But we were both so young…and I didn't…couldn't…'

His arms tightened when she stumbled, giving silent support. Oddly enough, it was as though the rapture she'd found with Cade had opened a door she'd slammed shut years ago.

When he asked, 'How young?' she told him.

'Nineteen, and he was twenty-one. Far too young, my parents said, and they were so right, but…at first everything was like a romantic fairy tale. Only once we were engaged he wanted to make love, and he was bewildered—and hurt—when I couldn't…'

She stopped and took a deep breath. Possibly without realising it, Cade was stroking her back and the slight, slow caress was soothing something more than her laboured heartbeat.

In a soft, dragging voice she said, 'I still don't know why I froze every time. He was experienced—I wasn't his first lover. He said I was frigid. And I thought it was true because I was so certain I loved him. But I just couldn't relax…'

Cade said quietly, 'So he found some-one new?'

'Oh, no.' She swallowed. 'He tried everything… I think he saw my coldness as a challenge to his masculinity.'

She couldn't go on. Antony had been utterly determined to overcome her frigidity. Sex with him had become an ordeal of new techniques, new attempts at seduction—from watching pornography with her to licking chocolate from her body—in his efforts to discover the magic caress that would miraculously turn her into the willing, eagerly passionate partner he wanted.

His dogged efforts had only made her more tense, eventually creating a rift, one that had rapidly spiralled out of control.

Cade said quietly, 'That doesn't sound like love.'

In a low, shaken voice, she said, 'He got so angry—as though I was doing it deliberately. I didn't know how to handle it—' She stifled a laugh that sounded too much like a sob. 'I wanted to run home to my mummy and daddy like a little girl and have them make things all better for me.'

'But they weren't there for you.'

'They were dealing with an outbreak of dengue fever that was killing people.' Her voice strengthened. 'So of course I didn't tell them.'

'What happened?'

When she shivered his arms tightened around her again. Keeping her face hidden in his shoulder, she mumbled, 'We were fighting a lot…and he…in the end I told him I didn't want him and never would, and he…and he…' She stopped, unable to go on.

'It's all right.' In a tone so devoid of emotion it was more threatening than anger, Cade said, 'Let me guess. He raped you.'

Taryn shuddered. 'Yes,' she whispered, adding swiftly, 'Afterwards he was shattered. He said he still loved me, even though I'd turned him into a monster.'

Every muscle in Cade's big body tightened. 'And you believed that—that self-serving, righteous—' he paused before clearly substituting another word for the one that must have sprung to mind '—*rubbish*?'

'At first I did,' Taryn admitted quietly. 'And even when I realised he had no right—that he was responsible for what he did, I still believed...'

'That you were frigid,' he supplied when she couldn't go on, his voice hard with anger. 'Well, now you know you aren't. Far from being frigid, you're delightfully responsive, all any man could ask for. If he wasn't able to make you respond, it was probably because you sensed the propensity for violence in him. No man has the right to take out his frustration in rape. It's every bit as criminal and brutal as beating a woman.'

Something that had been wound tightly inside her for years eased, dissipated, left her for ever. She felt oddly empty, yet light and free.

More shaken than she'd ever been, she said, 'I don't know why I told you all this.'

'Feel better?'

She sighed. 'Yes. Thank you.'

Thank you for everything. Thank you for making a woman of me...

'You don't need to thank me,' he said abruptly.

'I've done nothing—you always had the capacity for passion. It was your bad luck you thought you loved someone who didn't know how to arouse it.'

'Stupidity, more like,' she murmured.

He laughed quietly. 'Who isn't stupid at nineteen?'

Comforted, she luxuriated in the heat of his body, the smooth lift and fall of his chest, the sensuous, languid delight of being there with Cade. The world righted, reassembled itself, and she yawned.

'Do you want me to stay?' he asked.

Taryn's acrobatic heart jumped in her breast. It was utterly stupid to feel that this was more important than making love with him; that his question even implied some tenuous commitment...

In a voice she hoped sounded lazily contented, she murmured, 'If you want to.'

His smile sizzled through her. 'At the moment I don't think I can move,' he said and stretched, his big, lithe body flexing before he settled himself back beside her. There was a note of humour in his tone when he finished, 'But if you'd rather sleep alone I'll make the effort. A little later.'

'Mmm.' Another yawn took her by surprise.

'Sleep now,' he said, tucking her against him again.

Taryn had never actually slept with anyone. She and Antony had always made love in his flat and afterwards she'd gone back to hers, but having Cade beside her felt so natural—so right—she drifted almost immediately into slumber.

Cade waited until her breathing became deep and regular before easing her free of his embrace and turning onto his back, folding his arms behind his head as he stared out into the soft silver-hazed darkness.

Only when she moved away from him did he look at her. Even through the netting, the light of the moon shone strongly enough to pick out the long, elegant line of her sleek body and burnish her skin to a pale ivory quite different from its daylight colour of warm honeyed cream.

His hooded gaze traced the curves of her breasts and waist, the pure line of her profile, the lips his kisses had made tender. Astonishingly, his senses stirred again, startling him.

She'd been a willing and lusty lover, her response deliciously sensual. Yet there had been that intriguing element of...not exactly shyness, more like delighted bewilderment when she'd unravelled in his arms.

Although he was still furious with the man who'd abused her, the realisation that no one else had been able to elicit that shuddering primal response produced a visceral, addictive kick of satisfaction.

Of course, the whole story could be a lie...

His instinctive vehement resistance to this possibility warned him he was on the brink of making a huge mistake—of forgetting the reason Taryn was with him. All he'd intended was to get closer to her, find out what made her tick, why she'd laughed at Peter's proposal—what had made Peter decide his life was no longer worth living if she wasn't in it.

But he'd let himself get sidetracked. Seducing her had not been part of the plan.

Unfortunately, he'd wanted her from the moment

he'd seen her. Worse than that, he'd let his hunger eat away at his self-control.

Had that happened to Peter? Was that why he'd killed himself—because she'd bled him dry and then left him?

Cade fought back a cold anger, realising with icy self-derision that he didn't want to picture Taryn in his brother's bed. Shocked to realise his hands had clenched into serviceable fists, he deliberately relaxed every muscle.

He wouldn't let such a stupid adolescent emotion as jealousy crumble his hard-won self-control.

Life had taught him that ignoring inconvenient or unpleasant facts and possibilities invariably led to foolish decisions and bitter consequences.

Why did the thought of Taryn responding to Peter with the same passion and heady desire she'd shown a few short minutes ago make him feel like committing some act of violence?

His mouth tightened. Because he'd allowed her to get to him. Somehow, in spite of everything he knew and suspected about her, he'd let down his guard.

A seabird called from above the palms, a

sorrowing screech that lifted the hairs on the back of his neck.

Ignore the damn bird, he thought grimly. Face facts.

Lust meant nothing—any normal man would look at Taryn's beautiful face and lithe body and wonder what she was like in bed. But he'd made love to her knowing—and ignoring—the fact she was the only person who knew what had driven Peter to take his life.

He needed to know the reason, and not just because he'd promised his mother he'd find out. For his own peace of mind.

He suspected Peter had always felt slightly inferior. It hadn't helped that he'd never been able to match Cade physically, or that after their father's frightening bout of cancer when Peter was at school both parents had tended to rely more and more on their elder son.

Certainly his brother's behaviour at university hadn't convinced them he was someone they could rely on. Revelling in the freedom, Peter had wallowed in everything college offered except the opportunity to study.

Cade frowned, remembering how worried their parents had been. Fortunately, his brother's discovery of talent as a sculptor had ended that period of dissipation. To everyone's surprise—possibly even Peter's—his interest had become his passion.

He'd been *good*. He might eventually have been great. To die without ever fulfilling his potential would have been bad enough, but to kill himself because a pretty thief laughed at his offer of love and marriage was a bitter travesty.

Cade took a harsh breath, freezing when Taryn moved beside him. He waited until she settled her long legs and tried not to think of them around his hips, to banish from his mind the way she'd given herself utterly to desire.

To him…

His inglorious satisfaction at that thought both shamed him and brought his body to full alert again.

Staying in her bed had been a stupid, passion-addled decision. As soon as she was sleeping soundly enough he'd leave. Until then, he'd concentrate on the fact that she'd almost certainly spent the money Peter had given her. If she still had any of it, she wouldn't have had to resort to a job in a dead-end village.

Perhaps she'd given it to her parents to finance a clinic or a hospital somewhere?

Angered by this futile attempt to provide an excuse, he stared unseeingly across the room.

Think logically, he commanded. It had to be a possibility; although he might think her parents had a very cavalier attitude towards her, she clearly didn't. She'd been very quick to defend them.

Possibly he could find out if an unexpected amount of money had arrived in her parents' coffers. He'd get someone onto it tomorrow morning.

A slight breeze shimmered through the white mosquito netting. Again Cade glanced across at the woman beside him. As though his gaze penetrated the veils of sleep, she murmured something and turned back to him. A lovely, sensuous enigma, she lay like a child, one hand under her cheek, her face calm except for a tiny half smile that curled her lips. Long coppery hair tangled across her shoulder, half covering her breasts.

Once again, Cade's body stirred into urgent hunger. He swung his legs over the side of the bed and stood up. Lashes fluttering, Taryn gave a little sigh, but her eyes remained closed and almost immediately she sank back into deeper sleep.

Moving with a noiseless tread, Cade scooped up his clothes and headed for the door before he could yield to the temptation to get back into the bed and stroke her into wakefulness, to make love to her again…

No, not to make love.

To have sex with her again, he reminded himself savagely, silently closing her bedroom door behind him.

Back in his own room, he threw his clothes onto a chair and strode across to the windows, pushing back the shutters to drag warm sea-tangy air into his lungs. It had seemed so simple, so logical to bring her to Fala'isi so he could study her more closely. Instead, he'd got himself into an emotional tangle.

No, not emotional. He was *not* in love with her. He didn't know what love was about, so whatever he was feeling right now was—irrelevant.

CHAPTER TEN

DAZED by memories and dreams, Taryn woke from the best sleep she'd experienced for months and smiled sleepily at the crooning of the doves outside. When she'd first heard them she'd been astonished at such a European sound here, but after only a few days they'd become an intrinsic part of Fala'isi for her.

She'd always remember them—along with last night.

Colour burned up through her skin. She was glad Cade had left before she'd woken, yet some weak part of her mourned his absence.

She flung the sheet back, stretching and wincing a little at the protest from rarely used muscles. Making love with Cade had been a considerably more athletic exercise than she was accustomed to.

He'd known exactly what to do to make her

body sing with desire, to waken that urgent, exquisite hunger, then send her soaring into an alternate universe where the only thing that mattered was sensual rapture.

She glanced at her watch, muttering as she leapt off the bed. A quick shower left her no time for memories; she pulled on a cool shift that seemed almost formal in this relaxed atmosphere, but had to summon her boldest face when she finally walked out of her room.

Only to find he wasn't there.

He'd written a note, about as personal as a legal document, telling her he'd be back some time in the afternoon. However, he left her with work to do.

It took her all morning to track down and collate the information he asked for, and when she'd finished she looked along the white coral path for any sign of him.

Nothing. The island drowsed in the bright glow of tropical heat. For once the feathery palm fronds were silent and still against a sky so blue and bold it hurt her eyes. Even the lagoon was too warm when she swam, its silky waters enervating rather than refreshing.

She met him on the shell path just after she'd rinsed off the salt water from her body. Although a *pareu* hid her wet bikini, his gaze kindled and he reached out to touch her shoulder but, to her disappointment, immediately let his hand drop.

'Enjoy your swim?' he asked.

'Very much, thank you.'

Sensation churned through her, exciting yet making her apprehensive. She'd never felt like this before—as though the world was fresh and new and infinitely alluring—and she didn't know how to deal with it. Would he expect her to be blasé and sophisticated?

He broke into her thoughts by saying abruptly, 'I've cancelled the trip to check out the fishing industry.'

After a startled upwards look, she nodded. 'OK.'

His black brows lifted. 'No protests? No insistence that you've been looking forward so much to it?'

She grinned. 'I'm not a liar, unless it's polite

white lies. And even then I try to avoid them if I can. I'd find the trip interesting, I'm sure, but business is business. And you're the boss so you get to make the decisions.'

They'd set off walking towards the *fale*, but he stopped in the brief shade of the palms and demanded, 'Is that how you think of me?'

When Taryn hesitated he said, 'The truth, Taryn.'

'Until yesterday,' she said, hoping he couldn't see that she was hedging.

'Just that?'

She sent him a level glance. 'Do you really want to know, or are you pushing me to prove that I always tell the truth?'

Emotion flashed for a moment in his gaze before his lashes came down. When they lifted again his gaze was steely and relentless. 'Both.'

'I don't like being tested,' Taryn said steadily and set off again, her emotions in turmoil. She didn't know what he wanted from her, but she certainly wasn't going to tell him that last night had changed her in some fundamental way.

If she did, he'd probably send her home.

Making love with him had been like setting off into dangerous, unknown territory with no map, no provisions and no equipment, furnished only with hope. Last night it had seemed simple and right. Today she was more wary. If she wanted to keep her heart free and unscathed, she suspected she should be making plans to get back to New Zealand.

And knew she wouldn't.

Abruptly, she said, 'You already know that I found you very attractive right from the start. But until we changed the rules yesterday I did my best to regard you as my employer.'

'And now?'

He was ruthlessly pushing for something from her, an answer to a question she didn't understand.

Half exasperated, half distressed, she said, 'I have no claim on you, just as you have none on me. We both know this is a temporary arrangement between us. If you want to forget about it, tell me and we'll call it quits.'

And held her breath, feeling as though her whole future depended on his answer.

Cade said in a voice that brooked no argument, 'I shouldn't have started this out here. We'll talk once we're back in the *fale*.'

In the cool dimness of the living room he glanced at the pile of papers on the table and then, blue eyes hooded, examined her face. 'I want to make sure that the fact that I'm your employer had no bearing on your charming surrender last night.'

'I haven't been to bed with any other of my employers,' she said stiffly, obscurely hurt.

'I didn't intend to insult you,' he said, his voice hard. 'I certainly didn't mean to imply that you slept with all—or any of—your employers. I just wanted to make absolutely sure that you didn't feel pressured into making love.'

Taryn shook her head vigorously. 'No.'

And stopped, because anything more might reveal too much. But couldn't he tell that she'd surrendered wholeheartedly, with everything she had, everything she was?

Once again that flinty gaze probed hers for long heart-stopping seconds, until he seemed to relax and drew her towards him. Almost abstractedly, he murmured, 'You're the only employee I've ever made love to.'

His head came down and he kissed her throat, saying against her skin, 'You taste like the sea, sun-warmed and salty, scented with flowers and the wind.'

Unable to hold back, she turned her face into his and they kissed, and he found the knot of her *pareu* and it dropped in a wet heap on the floor, leaving her only in her bikini. Cade made a deep noise in his throat and his arms locked around her. Without further resistance, she lifted her face for his kiss, body pressed to body as desire— torrid and compelling—flashed between them.

'And you taste of you,' she said on a sigh when he finally lifted his head.

Taryn expected him to loosen his arms, but he didn't. Resting his cheek on her wet hair, he said, 'Not regretting anything?'

Regret? How could she regret the most wonderful experience of her life so far? Last night had been utterly magical, a revelation to her.

Was being a good lover a talent, something instinctive? How many women had Cade practised with to gain that mastery? Not only had he divined which parts of her were acutely sensitive to his touch, but he'd been slow and subtle and erotically compelling, seducing her until she'd had no thought for anything beyond the enchantment he worked on her willing body and mind.

'Not a thing,' she said huskily.

He smiled dangerously and let her go, but his grip slid down to fasten around her wrists so he could lift her hands to his mouth.

Tiny shivers chased the length of her spine as he kissed each palm. Be careful, some part of her warned. Be very careful. You don't want to lose your heart to him. Remember, he might want you but it's not going to last.

His tone amused, he said, 'Then we're suited in every way,' and kissed her properly again.

Joy fountained through Taryn. Once again, she felt the swift, piercing surge of desire, brazen as the tropical sun, and this time she had no forebodings, no fear about whether or not she was going to be able to respond. This time she could make love to Cade with complete confidence that the same rapture that had taken her to paradise the night before was waiting for her again.

'You'll get all wet,' she said against his throat.

'Mmm,' he murmured. 'Somehow, keeping dry is not a priority right now.'

'What is?'

He looked into her face with half closed eyes and the fierce smile of a hunter. 'Making it to a bed.'

They got there, but only just, and later, in a dreamy daze as she listened to him breathe beside her, Taryn decided she'd never been so happy before, never felt so completely at one with the world.

She drifted into sleep, but stirred when he got up. Opening her eyes, she smiled mistily at him, that flame of awareness beating high within her again at the sight of him, lean and bronzed and beautifully made, as powerfully built as he was desirable.

He dropped a kiss on her mouth but, before she could reach out and pull him down, he straightened. 'Dinner,' he said succinctly.

'Help, yes!' She swung her legs over the side of the bed and sat up. Tonight they were having dinner with the Chapmans.

Gaze darkening, Cade said, 'Don't move—try not to even breathe—until I get out of the room.'

Thrilled by her effect on him, she obediently froze.

Laughing softly, he left, scooping up his clothes as he went.

I'm in love with him, she thought, suddenly assailed by a wild mixture of apprehension and delight. *I'm in love with Cade Peredur.*

No, that was just foolish post-coital bliss scrambling her brain. She straightened her shoulders; she was perfectly content with the rules they'd made. Love had nothing to do with this. Eventually, they'd go their separate ways and she'd grieve for a while and miss him like crazy.

She'd gone into their affair with her eyes open and when it ended she'd get on with real life, grateful to Cade for showing her that she was a normal woman who could make love with abandon and joy.

So she'd accept this fantasy interlude for what it was—an enchantment that would end once they left the seductively sensuous lure of the tropics. And, if all went well, she might one day find a man she could both desire and truly love, one who'd love her.

Dinner with the Chapmans was fun; Fleur was an excellent hostess, Luke an interesting man with the same inbuilt authority that marked Cade. Afterwards, they drank coffee and watched the moon rise over the ocean, and Cade mentioned her parents.

'They do magnificent work,' Luke Chapman said. 'I believe they've just acquired a new yacht.'

Taryn nodded. 'A much bigger one. They've had it converted into a sort of mini-hospital and it's working well, but Dad's next project is to find the finance for a shore-based hospital on one of the outlying islands. And, after that, they want to set up a trust that will help local people study as nurses and doctors. He wants to make sure that when he and Mum retire—if they ever do—they leave a working system behind.'

'Big ambitions,' Luke observed.

'And expensive ones,' Cade supplied. 'Where do they find the money to keep going?'

Taryn laughed, then sighed. 'So far it's been mainly donations. Dad's quite shameless when it comes to asking for it.'

'That's a chancy, hand-to-mouth way for a charity—especially a private one—to exist. Setting up the new yacht must have cost them a packet,' Cade said.

'They were lucky—they got a big donation at just the right time.' Sadness struck her at the thought of Peter, who'd been so insistent on donating it.

And, emboldened by the Chapmans' obvious interest, she looked directly at their host. 'They want something along the lines of the health service you have here.'

Which led to further discussion. The Chapmans made no promises but, as she and Cade left, Luke said, 'I'll give you the name of the man who runs our health service. Your father could do worse than get in touch with him.'

Out of earshot, Cade said thoughtfully, 'You're a good daughter.'

Flushing, Taryn replied, 'My parents deserve all the help they can get.'

He said nothing more and she wondered whether he too was thinking of helping her parents. If so, perhaps they might keep in touch…

Don't, she told herself in sudden anguish. Don't hope for anything more. It wasn't going to happen, and wishing for it would only make it harder to recover.

Because now her heart was involved. Oh, she'd tried so hard to ignore it but, as they'd talked over the coffee table, she'd looked across at Cade and *known* she loved him. The knowledge had pierced her like a sword—transcendent yet shattering. Life without Cade stretched before her, bleak as a desert.

She looked up into a sky so brightly lit by the moon the stars were tiny pinpricks against black velvet. No sign of fruit bats, she thought wistfully.

If it hadn't been for that low-flying one, would Cade have ever kissed her?

Another question she couldn't answer.

Back in the *fale*, Cade glanced at his watch. 'I'm expecting a call from London in a few minutes, so I'll say goodnight now.'

It was like a blow to the heart. She felt her expression freeze and said hastily, 'Oh! Goodnight then.'

He surprised her by kissing her lightly, an arm round her shoulder holding her without passion.

'Sleep well,' he said and left her, walking into his room.

But, once there, he stood indecisively for a few moments, looking around as though he'd never seen the room before.

Every instinct was telling him to get out. He was in too deep and tonight he'd slipped over some invisible boundary, one he hadn't known existed. The whole evening had been—he struggled to find the right word and could only come up with *satisfying*. Satisfying in some deep, unplumbed way that scared the hell out of him.

He was falling and, if he didn't stop the process, he had no idea where he'd land. Damn it, it had been a quiet dinner with a couple he called friends, yet for some reason he'd accessed a level of—again, he searched for a word, finally settling on *contentment*—that still clung to him.

Contentment! He got to his feet and paced the room, angular face dark with frustration. Contentment was for the old, those with no further ambitions to pursue. He had plenty.

Yet, sitting under that voluptuous moon, watching the way its aura cooled Taryn's red hair and turned her skin to satin, listening to the low music of her laughter, he'd found himself thinking that life could hold nothing more for him.

Making love to her had been the most stupid thing he'd ever done.

No, bringing her to Fala'isi was that; their lovemaking had only compounded a problem he'd refused to face. Still didn't want to face.

There was only one thing to do. Before he lost his head and did something irretrievable, he had to tell her who he was, and what he wanted from her.

Surprisingly, Taryn slept well, waking next morning to sunlight and the muted coo of the doves against the slow thunder of the distant waves against the reef. And an aching emptiness because last night Cade had left her alone.

When she emerged, Cade was standing beside the pool, talking into his phone. He glanced up when he heard her, nodded and strode to the other end of the pool, the tension in his powerful back and lean, strong body warning her that something had gone wrong.

The terrace table had been set for breakfast for two, so she poured herself some coffee and spooned passionfruit pulp over golden slices of papaya.

She couldn't hear what Cade was saying, but his tone echoed his body language. He was angry.

When he strode over she asked a little warily, 'Trouble?'

'Problems.' Dismissing them, he sat down opposite her and examined her face, his expression flinty. 'All right?'

'Of course,' she said automatically. Much more than all right, in fact. Her heart was singing and every cell in her body responded with pleasure to the sight of him. 'Is there anything I can do?'

'No—just a business rival thinking that being on the other side of the world means I'm not keeping my eye on the kitchen. However, there is something I must tell you,' he said shortly. 'Did Peter Cooper ever tell you he had a brother?'

Taryn's spoon clattered into her plate. Searching his face, she swallowed. Nothing showed in the grey-blue eyes but an icy determination. 'Yes,' she answered automatically.

'Did you know I am—was—his brother?'

Taryn had never fainted in her life but, as she felt the colour drain from her skin, she thought dizzily that this was going to be the first time.

He said abruptly, 'Put your head down.' And, when she didn't move, he got to his feet and swivelled her chair around so he could push her head below her heart. The heavy, sick feeling beneath her ribs dissipated but she couldn't think—couldn't even make sense of the words jumbling through her mind.

After a few seconds the dizziness faded and she croaked, 'Let me up—I'm all right.'

'Sure?' He released her, watching her as she straightened.

After one look at his controlled face, she asked inanely, 'How can you be his brother? You don't have the same name.'

He shrugged. 'I went to the Coopers when I was five. Peter was born four years later.'

Taryn blinked, her mind seizing on this because she didn't dare—not yet—ask why he hadn't told her right at the start who he was.

'I see.' Heart twisting at the thought of what he must have endured as a child, she concentrated with fierce determination on the cluster of hibiscus flowers in the centre of the table.

She'd never be able to enjoy their showy vividness again without remembering this moment. *Peter's brother.* Cade was Peter's foster-brother.

Taryn believed in coincidences, but not where Cade was concerned.

Cade made things happen. He must have known that she and Peter had been friends.

Had he deliberately tracked her down? Was his lovemaking a sham? *Why?*

Pain sliced through her, so intense she hugged herself, trying to force the mindless agony away. When she trusted herself to speak again, she asked quietly, 'Why didn't you tell me this when we first met?'

His eyes narrowed into flinty shards. In a tone that almost brought her to her feet, ready to run, he said, 'Because I wanted to find out what sort of woman you were.'

'Why?' Every breath hurt, but she had to know.

He said evenly, 'I wanted to know what the woman who laughed at his proposal was like.'

Taryn almost ducked as though avoiding a blow. White-faced and shaking, she had to force herself to speak. 'How...how did you know that?'

His beautiful mouth tightened—the mouth that had brought her such ecstasy.

'How I know doesn't matter. Are you surprised that I should want to know why he killed himself?'

Dragging in a sharply painful breath, she reached deep into her reserves to find strength—enough strength to force herself up so she faced him, head held high.

'No,' she said quietly. 'Do you think I don't regret laughing? That I don't wish I could go back in time and change how I reacted? I thought he was joking.'

'Men do not *joke* about proposing,' he said between his teeth, making the word sound obscene. 'Why the hell would you think that?'

'Because we didn't have that sort of relationship,' she cried. 'We were friends—good friends—but we'd never even kissed.'

Stone-faced, he asked, 'Never?'

Firming her jaw, she admitted, 'The occasional peck on the check, that's all. Nothing beyond that. In fact, I thought—' She stopped.

'Go on,' he said silkily.

She swallowed. 'I thought he had a lover... There was a woman...' She stopped and forced her brain to leash the tornado of emotions rioting through her. 'Or that he might be gay.'

Cade looked at her, his expression kept under such rigid discipline she had no idea what he was thinking.

'He wasn't. Far from it.' He made a sudden, abrupt gesture, his control splintering. 'So if he never made a move on you, never showed that he wanted you, never indicated he might be in love with you, why the *hell* did he propose?'

'I don't know,' she said wretchedly. 'I really did think he was joking. And I was so taken aback— so startled—I laughed. Until I realised he was serious. I never thought… I *still* find it hard to believe he was in love with me.'

'I'm finding everything you've said hard to believe,' he said in a level judicial voice. 'I know—knew—my brother better than anyone, and he wouldn't have rashly proposed to a woman he wasn't sure of. Peter wasn't one for wild impulses.'

Taryn opened her mouth, then closed it again.

Harshly, Cade said, 'Tell me what you were going to say.'

When she hesitated, he commanded in a tone that sent a cold shiver scudding down her spine, *'Tell me.'*

'Just that as a brother you might have known him well, but as a man…how much time did you spend with him? He could be impulsive. And before he—'

'Killed himself,' Cade inserted when she couldn't go on.

'Before he died,' she went on bleakly, 'he was ecstatic at scoring that wonderful commission. It meant so much to him. He told me it validated everything he'd done before, and that he'd finally make his family proud of him. He was so happy planning the sculpture, so eager to get on with the work—almost crazy with delight.'

Shocked, she realised she was wringing her hands. She stopped, reasserted control and said without thinking, 'I swear, killing himself was the last thing on his mind.'

'Because he believed you loved him,' Cade said ruthlessly. 'When he proposed, what did you say to him?'

CHAPTER ELEVEN

TARYN flinched when she met Cade's—*Peter's brother's*—hooded, pitiless eyes. 'After I laughed, do you mean?' she asked on a half sob. 'I told him that although I liked him very much and valued him enormously as friend, I wasn't in love with him.'

'And what did he say to those noble sentiments?'

Colour flamed the length of her cheekbones, then faded into an icy chill. 'He said he hoped I'd always remember him as a good friend.'

'And it didn't occur to you he was saying goodbye?' he demanded incredulously.

'Of course not.' Then she said swiftly, 'Well… yes. Yes, of course I realised that our *friendship* was over. His proposal changed everything—and I was going back to New Zealand in a few hours.

But…if he loved me, why did he leave it so late to propose?'

Cade said nothing and she went on in a low, subdued voice, 'I did…I did love him, but not the way he wanted me to, and I still can't…'

Cade remained emphatically silent while she gulped back her emotions, eventually regaining enough self-possession to say in a voice drained of all colour, 'I d-don't know what I could have done to help him.'

'Nothing.' He was watching her so closely she took a step backwards. In a level voice, he said, 'Although offering to return his money might have made some difference to his decision to kill himself.'

'Money?' She flushed when she realised what he was talking about. 'It had already gone to my parents. It was used to fit out the new yacht—and he wanted to give it to Mum and Dad, Cade. If you believe nothing else, believe that. He insisted on sending it to them.'

He shook his head. 'Not that—I know he donated it to your parents. As I said last night—you're a good daughter.'

Now she understood what he'd meant—and why he'd left her alone last night.

Numbly, she listened to him continue, shrivelling inside when he went on, 'Peter had every right to give his money to whoever he wanted to. No, the money I'm talking about is the rest of his advance for the sculpture he was commissioned to produce.'

His words rang senselessly in her ears, jangling around her head in meaningless syllables. She stared at him, met penetrating eyes that judged and assessed every tiny muscle flickering in her face.

'What are you talking about?' she asked numbly.

He lifted one eyebrow to devastating effect. 'Don't be coy, Taryn. As well as the donation for the clinic, Peter gave you a large chunk of that advance. Where is it?'

Deep inside her, some fragile, persistent hope shattered into shards, dissolved into nothingness, leaving behind a black bitterness and misery.

Cade had deliberately targeted her, tracked her down and made love to her—because he thought she'd taken money from Peter. A large amount of money. Peter had gleefully told her how much it was, and that it was to be used to buy the materials for his sculpture.

Everything Cade had done, he'd done because he was convinced she was a thief. He'd brought her here, made love to her, given her such joy— and it was all false, all lies...

Trying to speak, she discovered that her throat had closed. Her stomach turned and she clapped a hand over her mouth.

He said, 'Stay there.'

Taryn closed her eyes, shielding her misery from him. She heard a clink and felt a glass of water being put into her hand.

'Drink it up,' he advised.

Their fingers touched and, in spite of everything, a jolt sparked through her. Dear God, she thought wearily, how could her body betray her like that when she now knew exactly what he thought of her—a liar and a common thief?

She wished she could summon righteous anger at being so badly misjudged, but her only emotion was a deep, aching grief for a fantasy that had turned into a dark nightmare.

Although she was sure she'd choke if she tried to drink the water, her throat was so dry and painful she forced several gulps down.

'Thank you,' she said hoarsely, wishing he'd step back. He was too close, and she...she was as broken as though the very foundations of her world had been cut from under her.

Clutching the glass in front of her like a pathetically useless shield, she said, 'I don't have anything of Peter's—certainly not his money.'

'Taryn, if you don't have it, who does?'

He spoke quite calmly and for a brief, bewildered second she wondered if indeed—somehow—she did have the money.

Then sanity returned, and with it some courage. 'I don't know,' she said. Her voice wobbled, so she swallowed and tried again. 'All I know is that he didn't give me any money. I'll furnish you with the records of my bank account so you can see for yourself.'

His lashes drooped. 'I want to see them, although if you took it you've had plenty of time to stash it away and cover your tracks.' He waited for a second and when she remained silent went on, 'It will be much easier if you just tell me where it's gone. Once it's returned, we'll forget about it.'

Fighting back against shock and fear and disillusionment, she drained the glass and set it down. She looked up, measuring him like a duellist of old, sensing that once again he was testing her, assessing her reactions to discern whether she'd stolen the money.

In other words, he wasn't sure.

The thought acted like a stimulant, but she forced herself to repress the wild hope that burst into life. Although her thoughts were still far from coherent, she said as calmly as she could, 'I swear to you, Peter didn't give me a cent all the time we knew each other.'

'Taryn, every financial transaction leaves a paper trail.'

When she shrugged, he finished softly, 'I can find those trails.'

It was a threat, but now she'd found a few shreds of composure she recognised it for an empty one.

'You'll discover that there's nothing to find. Cade, you'll never know how sorry I am that Peter's dead, and how sorry I am that I laughed when he proposed. I have that on my conscience, but not the loss of his money. And now I want to go home.'

Home? She didn't have a home, but if she didn't get away from Cade soon she'd crack. Now that she knew the depths of his betrayal, she couldn't bear to stay anywhere near him—let alone pretend they were lovers.

'We'll be leaving tomorrow,' he said inflexibly. 'Until then, I'll expect you to behave as you have been.'

'You must be joking!' she burst out, incredulous at his arrogant command.

'Far from it.' And when she started to speak again he said, 'You won't get off the island without my permission so don't try it.'

She stared at him, met an implacable gaze. He had to be lying—yet, perhaps not. Fleur Chapman might be a warm, compassionate woman, but her husband had the same air of effortless, uncompromising authority that marked Cade. They were also good friends.

And there were her parents—if the Chapmans were thinking of helping their mission, she didn't dare put that in question. Quietly, she said, 'Very well, I'll work for you, but that's all.'

'That's all I want,' he returned.

He turned away, stopping when she said, 'Why did you wait until now to tell me this?'

Without looking at her, he said, 'It had gone far enough.'

And he strode out of the room.

Taryn made sure she was in bed when he came back in the warm tropical night. Working had given her mind something to do—something other than returning endlessly to that moment when Cade had accused her of stealing money from Peter and stripped away her foolish, self-serving illusions.

Except that in bed, faced with the truth, her mind refused to allow sleep. Endless, scattered, anguished thoughts tumbled through her mind until she forced herself to accept that she couldn't love Cade. He'd deceived her and seduced her.

Actually, he hadn't seduced her. Besotted idiot that she was, she'd met him more than halfway there.

But she had too much pride to love a man who could deliberately lie to her—even though she accepted he had good reason to find out what had killed his brother.

Most nights a sighing breeze kept the mosquito nets breathing in and out, but tonight the sultry heat—and what felt perilously like a broken heart—kept her wide-eyed and sleepless.

On a half sob, she thought Cade had caused her more wakeful hours than anyone else in her life.

A pang of exquisite pain made her catch her breath. More than anything, she wanted to be able to blank him out, forget she'd ever met him, ever seen him. The memories hurt too much.

So she set her mind to the mystery of Peter's missing advance. He'd splashed money around a bit once he'd gained the commission, but he hadn't been extravagant. Certainly not enough to have spent it all...

She was still mulling this over when she heard

Cade come into the *fale*. Her breath locked in her throat and her lashes flew up. For a few ridiculous seconds she hardly dared breathe, but of course he didn't knock on her door.

Once she left Fala'isi and Cade, surely she'd get over this aching emptiness, this sense of loss and loneliness, of being betrayed by hopes she hadn't even recognised?

Driven by a searing restlessness and a heart so sore it felt like an actual physical pain, she got up and walked across to the window. It took her some time to realise that Cade was out there in the tropical night, a tall, dark form standing beside the pool.

Still, so still, as though he couldn't move…

Moonlight shimmered across the arrogant planes of his face, picking out in silver the sweeping strength of bone structure, the straight line of his mouth. Tears burned behind Taryn's eyes, clogged her throat. She blinked them back, focusing on the object Cade held in his hand.

A flower, she realised when he turned it and light glimmered across its silken petals. A hibiscus bloom. What intrigued him so much about the blossoms?

Wincing, she saw him throw it down as he had done before. Then she froze when he suddenly stooped and picked up the flower. Hardly daring to breathe, she watched him walk towards the *fale*.

Her breath sighed out slowly and she turned and made her way back to her bed, too heartsore to do more than wonder why he'd bothered to pick up the flower…

Eventually exhaustion claimed her, but only to dream, and wake with a start to wonder why her unconscious mind had brought her images of a friend of Peter's, famous for her artistic installations.

Peter had respected Andrée Brown as an artist and enjoyed her acid wit, but they'd had an odd, edgy relationship. Sometimes Taryn had suspected he and Andrée were lovers, and wished she could like the woman more. She'd found her heavy-going, a nervy, almost neurotic woman who lived for her art and made no secret of her disdain for people without talent.

Grimacing into the humid air, Taryn used every technique she could remember to calm her mind and woo the oblivion of sleep. But when it arrived it was disturbed by chaotic, frightening dreams so that she woke in the morning unrefreshed and heavy-eyed.

Work was penance; treating Cade with cool dispassion was hell. Doggedly, she plugged through the day, even went to the beach in the late afternoon when she judged everyone would be inside preparing for drinks before dinner.

Soon she'd be back in New Zealand; she'd never have to see Cade again, and this heavy grief that had lodged in her heart would fade. People recovered from the most appalling things; she'd recover too.

She had to…

Shaded by palms, Cade watched her swim towards shore, long arms stroking effortlessly through the water. When she stood, the westering sun kindled an aura of gold from the glittering sheets of water that poured from her. She looked like Venus rising from the Mediterranean, slender and lithe and radiant, no sign of stress in her lovely face, her hair a sleek wet cloak of red so dark it was almost crimson.

Hot frustration roiled through him. Had he just made the biggest mistake in his life?

His jaw tightened as she stooped to pick up her towel. In spite of everything, heat flared through him. Damn the woman; he'd spent most of last night lying awake, remembering how sweetly, how ardently she'd flamed in his arms.

In spite of everything, he couldn't reconcile the laughing, valiant woman he'd come to know with the woman he knew her to be.

His cell phone stopped him just as he was about to step out onto the hot sand. He said something fast and low, but the call was from his PA in London. Today was the day they were to get the results of a further series of tests his PA's three-year-old had endured.

'Yes,' he barked into the phone.

He knew the instant his PA spoke. Instead of the heavy weight of fears of the past month or so, his tone was almost buoyant. 'It's not—what we feared.'

'Thank God,' Cade said fervently. 'What's the problem?'

He listened for a minute or so as Roger told him what lay ahead for little Melinda. When the voice on the other side of the world faded, he said, 'So it's going to be tough, but nowhere near as bad as it could have been.'

'No.'

'OK, take your wife and Melinda to my house in Provence and stay there for a week. Get some sun into all of you.' He cut short his PA's startled objection. 'I refuse to believe you can't organise someone to take your place. I won't be back for another week, so things can ride until then. And buy Melinda a gift from me—something she's been wanting.'

He overrode Roger's thanks, but fell silent when his PA asked urgently, 'Have you heard from Sampson?'

'No.' Not since the investigator he'd set to track down the money from Peter's account had come to a dead end.

Cade stiffened as the tinny voice on the other end of the phone said, 'He rang on Thursday to say he might have something for you in a couple of days.'

An odd dread gripping him, Cade glanced at his watch, made a swift calculation and said, 'OK, thanks. And enjoy Provence.'

He stood looking down at the face of his phone, then set his jaw and hit the button that would get him Sampson. As the investigator began to speak, his intent expression turned from hard discipline to shock, and then to anger. Swinging around as he listened, he strode back to the *fale*, the cell phone pressed to his ear.

An hour or so later, Taryn walked reluctantly into the *fale*, a *pareu* draped around her from armpit to ankle, only hesitating a moment when she realised Cade was already there.

He said harshly, 'I have something to tell you. Something about Peter.'

'I don't want—' She stopped, her eyes widening. He looked—exhausted. A fugitive hope died into darkness. It took her a moment to summon enough strength to say quietly, 'What is it?'

He closed his eyes a second, then subjected her

to an unreadable examination. 'Did you know he was a drug addict?'

Shock silenced her, leaving her shivering. She put out a shaking hand and clutched the top of a chair, bracing herself while Cade waited, his face held under such rigid restraint she couldn't discern any emotion at all.

She whispered, 'No. Oh, no. Are you sure?'

'Yes. I've just been talking to the man I got to investigate the whereabouts of Peter's advance.' He paused, then said in a voice she'd never heard before, one thick with self-disgust, 'You'd better sit down.'

'I'm all right,' she said automatically. 'Go on.'

But he shook his head. 'Sit.'

And because her head was whirling and she felt nauseated, she obeyed, but said immediately, 'You can sit too.'

He said, 'I feel better standing.'

Taryn swallowed. 'All right.'

But he sat down anyway.

Slowly, painfully feeling her way, she whispered, 'I hate to say it, but it makes sense. Peter was mercurial—in tearing good spirits one day, then in the depths the next. I thought it was artistic temperament—made even more so when he got that commission. And asking me to marry him was so out of the blue! He was a great, good friend, but there had been nothing…nothing like…'

Nothing like the instant, unmistakeable reaction between you and me. A glance at Cade's stern face made her remember that only she had felt that wild erotic response.

Stumbling a little, she went on, 'Just nothing. Which was why I thought he had to be joking.'

Would Cade believe her now? She held her breath, her heart thumping so heavily in her ears she had to strain to hear his reply.

'He wasn't joking,' he said roughly. 'He loved you.'

But Taryn shook her head. 'He never made the slightest approach—never touched me except for the odd kiss on the cheek—the sort of kiss you'd give a child.'

'I imagine he was afraid to let you get too close in case you found out about his addiction.' Cade spoke with a control that almost scared her. 'And, although I can't be sure, I suspect he began to hope that if you married him he'd be able to beat the addiction.'

Taryn drew in a ragged breath, grateful he'd made her sit. 'It would never have got that far,' she said numbly. 'I loved him too, but not—' She stopped again, because she'd been so lost in Peter's private tragedy she'd almost blurted out *not like I love you.*

'Not in a sexual way,' she finished, acutely aware of his probing gaze. 'But, oh, I *wish* I'd known. I might have been able to help him. At the very least, I'd have known not to laugh when he proposed…'

'He would have been ashamed of his weakness,' Cade said.

'If I'd understood, I wouldn't have let him down so badly.' The words were wrenched from a depth of pain she could hardly bear.

Cade said, 'He didn't tell anyone.' He paused before saying without inflection, 'Our parents knew what addiction could do, and not only to the one with the problem. My birth mother was an addict—they'd seen what living with her had done to me. When I arrived at their house I was feral—wild and filthy and barely able to function on any level but rage. They worked wonders with nothing more than uncomplicated love and fortitude and their conviction that there was some good in me.'

She made a slight sound of protest and he went on harshly, 'It's the truth. They fostered me because they were told they'd never be able to have children. Peter was their miracle, but it appears he always felt they loved me more than him.'

He'd withheld so much about himself, so much she'd longed to know. The telling of it was clearly painful and now she wished he didn't feel obliged to. 'I'm so sorry,' she whispered.

'Damn it, I don't know why,' he said with a hard anguish that wrung her heart. 'I just don't know.'

But Taryn thought she understood. When he compared himself to Cade's compelling character and the success he'd achieved, Peter must have felt inferior.

As though driven, Cade got to his feet, moving awkwardly for so lithe a man. For once he seemed unable to find the right words. 'I thought we had a good relationship, but it appears it was not. He didn't come to me for help because he resented me.'

'No,' she said swiftly. This was something she could give him—possibly the only thing he'd take from her.

She steadied her voice. 'Whenever he spoke of you there was no mistaking his affection. He never said your name—it was always *my brother*—but he told me little incidents of his childhood, and he always spoke of you with love. He might have felt he couldn't measure up to you, Cade, but he did love you.'

He got to his feet and strode across the room as though driven by inner demons. 'Life would be a hell of a lot easier without love. It complicates things so damned much,' he said angrily. Then, as though he'd revealed far too much, he continued, 'I owe you an apology.'

Taryn's breath locked in her throat. If only he'd tell her he'd really wanted her, that it hadn't all been a fantasy...

One glance at his face told her it wasn't going to happen.

He went on in a cool, deliberate tone, 'I should have made sure of my facts before I taxed you with stealing the money. It's no excuse that I didn't want to believe it, but no one else seemed close enough to him to be a suspect. And he'd given you the money for your parents.'

He hesitated, and she waited with her breath locked in her throat.

But he finished, 'From what the investigator has discovered, it probably all went to pay off drug debts.'

Yet another thing to blame himself for, she thought bleakly, once more faced with a situation she was unable to help, unable to do anything but watch him with an anguish she didn't dare reveal.

In a softly savage voice that sent shudders down her spine, he said, 'That supplier will be out of business very soon—just as soon as I find out who he is.'

'I might be able to help there,' Taryn said impulsively, immediately regretting her statement when he swung around, eyes narrowing. Choosing her words carefully, she said, 'Peter had a friend—an artist he respected—but it was a difficult relationship. Intense and vaguely antagonistic...'

As she spoke, she suddenly realised why she'd dreamed of the other woman. Torn, she hesitated.

'What was his name?' Cade demanded.

Taryn made up her mind and gave him Andrée Brown's name. 'I saw him handing her a wad of notes once. At the time I didn't think anything of it. It might have been perfectly innocent. Probably was.'

'But?' Cade said curtly.

She frowned, trying to put into words something that hadn't been suspicious but which she'd remembered. 'When he realised I'd seen he told me why—he had a perfectly logical reason, but his reaction was odd. Not for long, and not so much that I was at all suspicious, but just a bit *off*.'

Keen-eyed, he asked her to write the woman's name down, and when she hesitated once more, gave a hard, mirthless smile. 'Are you worried

I might hound her too? I never make the same mistake twice,' he said brusquely. 'Taryn, I've treated you abominably. Whatever I can do for you I'll do.'

'Nothing,' she returned automatically, chilled to the bone but holding herself together with an effort that came near to exhausting her.

He said harshly, 'Don't be a fool.'

Taryn's heart contracted, but she steadied her voice enough to be able to say, 'I accept your apology. You had what you thought were good reasons for your mistake—and I understand why you wanted to punish someone who took away your brother's hope.'

'He could have asked for help, booked himself into rehab.'

'Poor Peter,' she said, her voice uneven. 'Would you have helped him?'

'Of course.'

She believed him. 'And surely your parents wouldn't have turned against him?'

He wasn't nearly so quick to answer this time. 'At first they'd have been shocked and intensely disappointed, but they loved him. They'd have tried to help him. I had no idea he thought he'd failed them, and I'm sure they didn't suspect either. If they had, they'd have reassured him.'

Something about his words made Taryn say, 'You speak of them in the past tense.'

He shrugged. 'My father died of a heart attack two weeks after Peter's funeral, and my mother walked out in front of a car a few weeks later.' After a glance at her horrified face, he said immediately, 'No, she didn't intend to. She'll be in a wheelchair for the rest of her life.'

More than anything, Taryn longed to put her arms around him, give him what comfort she could. She didn't. His tone was a keep-off sign, a message reinforced by the jutting lift of his chin, taut stance and steely eyes.

She said quietly, 'I'm so sorry.'

'You have nothing to be sorry about.' As though he couldn't wait to be rid of her, he went on, 'I'll get you back to New Zealand straightaway.'

Within twelve hours she was in Aramuhu, listening to her landlord while he told her that the sleepout needed urgent repairs and she'd have to find somewhere else to live.

She nodded and must have appeared quite normal because he said, 'I'm sorry, Taryn. The roof's started to leak and I have to get it all repaired before the kiwi fruit pickers come in. You'll stay with us until you find somewhere else to live, of course.'

When he'd gone she sat down and let the slow, unbidden tears well into her eyes, farewelling the past, looking ahead at a future that loomed grey and joyless.

CHAPTER TWELVE

'TARYN, why won't you come with us?' Hands on her slender hips, her flatmate eyed her with exasperation. 'You're never going to get over The Mystery Lover by staying obstinately at home.'

Taryn's lazy smile hid the flash of pain that any mention of Cade always brought. 'I'm too tired to go halfway across Auckland for a concert—I walked up to the top of One Tree Hill this afternoon,' she said cheerfully. 'I'd be nodding off halfway through the first song.'

Isla grinned. 'You couldn't—the band's too loud. And you're not going to get over a broken heart by turning into a hermit.'

'I'm not a hermit,' Taryn told her. 'I'm an introvert. We enjoy being alone.'

Her flatmate wasn't going to be diverted. 'Piffle. It's just not *natural* for you to never go out with *anyone*.'

Taryn said with indignation, 'Stop exaggerating. I have gone out.'

'Friends don't count!' Isla flung her arms out in one of the dramatic gestures she did so well. 'Auckland has over a million people living here, half of them men, and quite a few of them looking for a gorgeous woman like you. But no, you ignore them all because you're still fixated on some man who did you wrong. You know how you're going to end up, don't you? You'll be an old maid, buying baby clothes for your friends' kids but never for your own. And it's such a waste because you're not only gorgeous, you're clever and nice as well, and you can cook and change a car tyre—the world *needs* your genes.'

'What's this about babies?' Taryn eyed her suspiciously. 'You're not trying to tell me you're pregnant, I hope?'

Isla snorted. 'You know better than that. Look, it's a fabulous night, just right for a concert in the Domain. I've got enough food and champagne to feed an army, and I happen to know that in our group there'll be one unattached, stunning man.

You'll love the whole thing. And it will do you good.'

'Thanks for suggesting it, but no.'

Isla cast her eyes upwards. 'OK, OK, but I'm not giving up—I'll get you out sooner or later, just see if I don't. And that's both a threat and a promise.'

She turned away to gather up the picnic basket and a wrap, adding over her shoulder, 'Still, at least you're no longer looking quite so much like a ghost. You had me really worried for a while.'

'I'm fine,' Taryn said automatically. 'Go on, off you go. Have fun.'

'That's a given. See you.' Isla disappeared down the passage of the elderly villa she shared with her two flatmates. The other one, a man, was away for the weekend. Taryn liked them both and got on well with them, grateful for their uncomplicated friendship, just as she was grateful for the job she'd found in one of Auckland's smaller libraries.

She heard the front door open and Isla's voice, startled and then welcoming. 'Yes, she's here.

In the living room—second door on the right. See you.'

Hastily, Taryn scrambled to her feet. She wasn't expecting a visitor.

The door opened and Cade walked in, somehow seeming taller than she remembered, she thought confusedly above the urgent clamour of her heart. Her stomach dropped and then a great surge of joy burst through her.

He stopped just inside the door, gaze hardening as he examined her. When her tension reached near-screaming point, he said, 'You've lost weight.'

Her head came up. Reining in the urgent need to feast her eyes on him, she said astringently, 'Thank you for that. *You* don't appear to have changed at all. How did you know where I live?'

'I've known since you got here,' he said, adding, 'and any changes in me are internal, but they're there. Are you going to ask me to sit down?'

Taryn cast a desperate glance around the room, furnished in cast-offs from Isla's parents, who were short. 'Yes, of course. The sofa, I think.'

Afraid to ask why he'd come, what he wanted, she sank into a chair, only to scramble up again. 'I'm afraid I haven't got anything to drink—not alcohol, I mean. Would you like some coffee? Or tea?' She was babbling and he knew it.

'No, thank you,' he said curtly. 'How are you?'

She managed to rake up enough composure to say, 'I'm fine. Thank you. Very well, in fact.' Struggling to control the wild jumble of emotions churning through her, she sat down again. 'How are things with you?'

Shrugging, he said in his driest tone, 'Fine. I thought you'd like to know that Peter's supplier is in custody now. And yes, the go-between was Andrée Brown—who cheated Peter by telling him the dealer was demanding more and more money. In effect, she drove him to his death. She's being investigated for fraud and drug trafficking.'

Taryn grimaced, relieved to have something concrete to fix on. 'I'm glad. It's been worrying me that Peter might never be avenged. It was kind of you to come and tell me.'

Cade said harshly, 'You deserved to know. And

I don't consider bringing them to account to be revenge—it's a simple matter of justice.'

Taryn realised every muscle was painfully tight, and that she was holding her breath. Forcing herself to exhale, she said, 'You said you always knew where I was—how?'

'I had someone keep an eye on you.' His mouth curved as he met her seething glance.

'Why?'

He shrugged. 'To make sure you were all right.'

Taryn didn't dare look at him in case the hope that bloomed so swiftly—so foolishly—was baseless. She said steadily, 'I'm all right, so you can go. Nothing can take away the fact that if I hadn't laughed at Peter and refused his proposal he'd probably be alive today.'

'It's no use going over what can't be changed.' He shrugged. 'You weren't to know—he must have gone to incredible lengths to hide his addiction from you—from everyone—as well as his dependence on that woman for them.'

Something shifted in Taryn's heart, and the

grief that had weighed her down since she'd left Fala'isi eased a little.

Uncompromisingly, he continued, 'We didn't understand how fragile he was because he took pains to prevent anyone from seeing it. Nobody could help him because he wouldn't let us see he needed it. We can wallow in guilt until we die, but it's not going to help Peter.'

Taryn swallowed. 'You sound so hard.'

He said harshly, 'I am hard, Taryn. I suspect the three years I spent with an addict mother toughened me. And the fact that she was an addict probably explains why Peter would have moved heaven and earth to keep me from finding out about his addiction.'

Taryn dragged in a deep breath. 'What happened to your mother?'

'She died soon after I went to the Coopers.'

'Your grandmother must have loved you,' Taryn said swiftly. 'Babies need love to be able to survive, and you not only survived, but you learned to love your foster-parents, and Peter when he arrived in the family. You're not that hard.'

He shrugged. 'That sort of love, yes, but until

I met you I wondered if I'd ever be able to love a woman in the way Harold Cooper loved Isabel.'

Inside Taryn wild hope mingled with bitter regret. Heat staining her cheeks, she met his unwavering regard with slightly raised brows. 'And after you met me?'

'I decided to use the attraction between us to get the information I wanted from you.' He stopped, then went on as though the words were dragged from him, 'But I made love to you because I couldn't stop myself.'

Her heart leapt and the pulse in her throat beat heavily, but she didn't dare let hope persuade her into more illusions. Mutely, she waited for whatever was to come next.

'When we were together I didn't think of Peter.' He spoke carefully, his face bleak yet determined. 'I was too concerned about hiding my response to you. Just by being yourself, you wrecked my logical plan to win your trust so you'd confide in me.'

'Logical?' she demanded, suddenly furious. 'Cold-blooded, more like.'

He frowned. 'Yes.' He paused, then said, 'I *am* cold-blooded. Cold-blooded and arrogant.'

In a shaken voice, she said, 'That's not true— you loved the Coopers. You set out on this...this charade...because you loved Peter. The time with your birth mother must have been horrific, but I'm so glad you had those early years with your grandmother and that the Coopers took you in. They must have been wonderful people.'

He said evenly, 'They were—my mother still is. And I don't want sympathy. But a background like that probably explains why—until I met you—I found it easier to talk of wanting rather than loving. It's no excuse. I had no right to do to you what I did. I should have told you who I was when we met.'

'Why didn't you?' she asked, almost against her will, and braced herself for his answer.

He said quietly, 'I expected someone like Peter's other girlfriends—like the lovers I've had, some- one charming and beautiful and chic and basi- cally shallow, I suppose. Instead, I saw a girl with a hose trying to put out a fire she had every reason to know would ultimately get away from her, possibly put her in danger. A woman who was beautiful under a layer of smoke and sweat, a woman who ordered me around.' He stopped, then said with an odd catch in his voice, 'A woman I could love. And every sensible thought went flying out of my head. Oh, I thought I was in control, but all I wanted was to get to know you, to find out what sort of person you were. I wouldn't—couldn't—accept that I'd fallen in love at first sight.'

Taryn went white. She stared at his controlled face, the only sign of emotion a tiny pulse flicking in his angular jaw. He *couldn't* have said what she thought she'd heard.

'I'm making a total botch of this,' he said curtly. 'I didn't believe I could love. But I did, even when I was telling myself that all I was doing was finding out why Peter had killed himself. And every day that passed I fell deeper and deeper in love with you without recognising it or accepting it. Although I told myself I needed to give you chances to talk about Peter, I really didn't want to know.'

He got to his feet. Unable to stay where she was,

she too stood, but couldn't move away from her chair. He paced across to the window and looked out at the rapidly darkening garden.

In a level voice that somehow showed strain, he said, 'I love you, Taryn. Even when I was accusing you—I loved you. I sent you back to New Zealand because I needed time to accept what I'd learned about my brother. And I needed to see my mother. But I came here because I couldn't stay away.'

For long moments she stared at him, his face drawn and stark, a charged tension leaping between them. He didn't move and she couldn't take a step towards him, held prisoner by caution that ached painfully through every cell in her body.

But she believed him, although it was too soon to feel anything other than relief, and a fierce desire to see everything out in the open after all the lies and secrets.

She said, 'That connection between us—I felt it too. I'd never have made love with you so quickly—so easily—if I hadn't somehow known that beneath the hunger and the excitement there was more. I didn't know what the *more* was, but it was always there, from the moment I saw you.'

He said her name on a long, outgoing breath, and covered the distance between them in two long strides.

But, half a pace away, he stopped and examined her face with a gaze so keen she had to fight the urge to close her eyes against it. His voice was deep and hard when he demanded, 'You're sure?'

'Yes,' she said with all her heart. 'Living without you has been a lesson in endurance, but it's made me utterly sure.' She gave a half smile and searched his beloved face. 'Are you?'

'Sure you deserve more than I can give you,' he said quietly. 'These past interminable weeks have shown me that without you my life is empty and useless, bleak and joyless. Taryn, I need you to make it complete.'

As though the admission opened some sort of channel he took that final step. Her eyes brimmed when his arms tightened around her to bring her against his lean, strong body.

'Don't,' he said in an anguished voice. 'Don't

cry, my love, my dearest heart. I don't deserve you, but I'll spend the rest of my life making you happy. I feel like an alien, dumped onto a strange, unknown planet with no support. It's like nothing I've ever experienced before. Once I'd realised I was falling in love, I was scared witless.'

She gave a little broken laugh. 'I understand the feeling. It's beyond comprehension. These past weeks have been...bleak. Hollow—just going through the motions.'

'Exactly. And, as I'm being honest about my feelings, I must admit I hoped I'd get over it.' His smile twisted. 'I tried to convince myself that loving you was an aberration, something that would die once you left. In fact, I felt like that feral five-year-old—at the mercy of something so much bigger than myself I had to protect myself in any way I could.'

'Oh, no,' she whispered, understanding for the first time why he'd fought so hard against this miraculous love.

'It's all right,' he soothed swiftly. 'And that's a stupid way of describing how I feel. How on earth do people deal with such an overwhelming, uncivilised need? I had to come and ask you if there was any hope for me.'

Every cell in her body cried out for the relief and joy of his arms around her.

But she said, 'I love you with all my heart, everything I am.' And pressed her fingers over his mouth when he went to speak. 'Cade—there's still the fact that, although I didn't intend it, I caused your brother's death.'

'You didn't,' he said simply. 'Possibly, he hoped you'd rescue him but, in the end, the decision to take his life was his, no one else's.'

'Your mother—'

'She knows I'm here, and why. She's not happy about this, and yes,' he said quietly, still holding her, 'I won't say that didn't affect me but, although I love her, this is none of her business. If you come to me, Taryn, I will do my best to make you happy, to make sure that you never regret it.'

His oddly formal phrases were enough to banish the final cowardly fear.

'Is it going to be so simple?' she asked softly.

'Because I will do my best to make you happy too. Is that all it takes?'

She felt his body stir against her and a leap of excitement pulsed through her.

'I hope so. It hasn't been easy for either of us,' he said quietly. 'I had to struggle with the knowledge that I'd done you a grave wrong, one I regret bitterly. Except that out of it has come this utter commitment to you—one without any reservations.'

Taryn's heart swelled and, lifting her face so she could kiss him, she said against his mouth, 'I love you so much.'

A year later, with small Teresa Rose Peredur sleeping in her arms, Taryn watched her husband come across the room.

Love misted her eyes. She'd never been so happy as in these past months. He'd supported her through her pregnancy and been with her during their daughter's birth, and he'd been wonderful in his dealings with her parents. Not only had he charmed them and won their respect, but he'd financed the trust they'd been trying to set up, so that by the time they gave up their practice there would be local doctors and nurses to take over.

Relations with his mother were still strained. She'd made her wheelchair the reason for not attending their wedding, and she wouldn't stay with them or visit them in the house they'd bought in Buckinghamshire, but Taryn hoped that time would ease Isabel Cooper's reservations.

'Our darling daughter is going to have your nose,' Taryn said happily, turning so Cade could look at the baby's face. 'It's stopped being snub and is turning into a definite aquiline.'

He laughed, scooping the baby from her arms. 'My poor little treasure,' he said in the voice he reserved for his daughter. 'Not that it isn't a perfectly efficient nose, but it's going to look a trifle odd in that beautiful face you've inherited from your mother.'

'It will give it character,' Taryn said firmly.

He laid the baby in her crib and came across and kissed his wife. 'My mother is coming up to London next week and asked if she could stay here a couple of nights,' he said, watching her keenly.

Elation filled her. 'I'm glad,' she said, hugging him. 'It's the first step, isn't it?'

'Yes, I think so,' he said without hesitation. 'She knows you a little better now, and she's accepted that whatever happened between you and Peter was not your fault.'

'I'm so glad.' It seemed inadequate to describe the relief she felt, but a glance at his face told her he understood.

He said, 'She'd been worried about him for some time, but he wouldn't confide in her. And she suspected drugs—that you might have introduced him to them. But when it came out at the trial that he'd been sleeping with that Brown woman, she accepted that your reaction to Peter's proposal wasn't as cruel as it seemed.'

Andrée Brown and the man who'd supplied her with drugs were both in prison.

Taryn glanced across at the sleeping baby. 'Even if we take Teresa to see my parents often, a child needs at least one grandparent close by. And your mother made such a brilliant job with you, I'm sure she can teach me a lot.'

He laughed and kissed her again, and they left

the nursery for their own room. As he started to change out of his business clothes, Cade said, 'Ready for next week?'

'Just about,' she said cheerfully.

Next week they were visiting her parents in Vanuatu. It would be the first time they'd seen their granddaughter, and she was excited.

'I thought you might like to drop in on the Chapmans,' he said. 'They've offered us the *fale* in Fala'isi.'

Where they'd first made love, where they'd married and spent their honeymoon...

'Lovely,' Taryn said, and hugged him exuberantly. Happiness expanded inside her, filling her with delight, but she said a little wistfully, 'It's a pity everyone can't have an ending like ours, isn't it.'

'Happy ever after?' he teased. 'My romantic love...'

'Only it's not an ending, is it,' she said soberly. 'It's a series of beginnings too, and they won't all be happy ones.'

'We'll deal with anything.' They exchanged a long look, one of perfect trust.

Heart swelling, Taryn nodded. 'Yes,' she said, smiling at his beloved arrogant face with perfect confidence. 'Whatever happens, we'll cope because we love each other. It really *is* that simple.'

MILLS & BOON PUBLISH EIGHT LARGE PRINT TITLES A MONTH. THESE ARE THE TITLES FOR JULY 2011.

A STORMY SPANISH SUMMER
Penny Jordan

TAMING THE LAST ST CLAIRE
Carole Mortimer

NOT A MARRYING MAN
Miranda Lee

THE FAR SIDE OF PARADISE
Robyn Donald

THE BABY SWAP MIRACLE
Caroline Anderson

EXPECTING ROYAL TWINS!
Melissa McClone

TO DANCE WITH A PRINCE
Cara Colter

MOLLY COOPER'S DREAM DATE
Barbara Hannay

MILLS & BOON PUBLISH EIGHT LARGE PRINT TITLES A MONTH. THESE ARE THE TITLES FOR AUGUST 2011.

JESS'S PROMISE
Lynne Graham

NOT FOR SALE
Sandra Marton

AFTER THEIR VOWS
Michelle Reid

A SPANISH AWAKENING
Kim Lawrence

IN THE AUSTRALIAN BILLIONAIRE'S ARMS
Margaret Way

ABBY AND THE BACHELOR COP
Marion Lennox

MISTY AND THE SINGLE DAD
Marion Lennox

DAYCARE MUM TO WIFE
Jennie Adams

WEB_M&B_RTL3 LP

MM

Discover Pure Reading Pleasure with

Visit the Mills & Boon website for all the latest in romance

Buy all the latest releases, backlist and eBooks

Find out more about our authors and their books

Join our community and chat to authors and other readers

Free online reads from your favourite authors

Win with our fantastic online competitions

Sign up for our free monthly eNewsletter

Tell us what you think by signing up to our reader panel

Rate and review books with our star system

www.millsandboon.co.uk

 Follow us at twitter.com/millsandboonuk

 Become a fan at facebook.com/romancehq